JANE'S
Dust

A TALE OF TALC, DECEIT, AND DEATH

DR. RONALD GORDON
& JOEL BROKAW

Copyright © 2022 Dr. Ronald Gordon & Joel Brokaw.

All rights reserved. No part of this book may be reproduced, stored, or transmitted by any means—whether auditory, graphic, mechanical, or electronic—without written permission of both publisher and author, except in the case of brief excerpts used in critical articles and reviews. Unauthorized reproduction of any part of this work is illegal and is punishable by law.

ISBN: 979-8-88640-646-7 (sc)
ISBN: 979-8-88640-647-4 (hc)
ISBN: 979-8-88640-648-1 (e)

Because of the dynamic nature of the Internet, any web addresses or links contained in this book may have changed since publication and may no longer be valid. The views expressed in this work are solely those of the author and do not necessarily reflect the views of the publisher, and the publisher hereby disclaims any responsibility for them.

One Galleria Blvd., Suite 1900, Metairie, LA 70001
1-888-421-2397

INTRODUCTION

This is a horror story of a very different kind. The monster is disguised and hidden, lurking in a white, dusty powder in our medicine chests in our homes—so ubiquitous, trusted, accepted, and engrained as a part of our daily routine for well over a century. This monster has been kept alive by lies, deceit, greed, privilege, arrogance, and a thirst for power. It is an unfolding human tragedy that is still among us, where medicine, corporate malfeasance, and the legal process collide. It follows a woman who dutifully trusted a product she used daily over most of her life and suffered grievous harm, and a corporate executive who dutifully fostered a lie to preserve his company's good name and profit at the cost of countless thousands of lives.

The authors of this story are Dr. Ronald Gordon and Joel Brokaw. Dr. Gordon is a pathologist at Mt. Sinai Hospital and Icahn School of Medicine at Mt. Sinai in New York, who is one of the world's leading experts in mesothelioma caused by talc. Joel Brokaw is a *New York Times* best-selling collaborator. Their work draws on more than three hundred court cases (where Dr. Gordon has served as an expert witness) that have pitted cancer victims against a few of America's most powerful corporations. The authors have taken poetic license to fictionalize the characters in this book based on true-life composites drawn from many of these cases. But it is not exaggerated, embellished, or varnished; it is the reality faced by many thousands of people, some of whom may be our family members, neighbors, or friends in our communities.

Every horror story leaves us with a cautionary tale. This one is no different.

Chapter 1

The last cars had pulled away only minutes before from the cemetery located on a green, rolling hillside overlooking a congested freeway. As the setting sun dipped to illuminate the Southern California haze, two workers clad in dark blue overalls put the finishing touches on the gravesite, smoothing out and packing down the remaining soil over the coffin.

A dozen family members had attended the private graveside service, the workmen keeping well in the background, waiting beside their equipment carts. Just as they had on several other burials that day, they worked methodically to inter the coffin, finishing up by spreading a temporary carpet of green artificial grass. It would cover the gash of brown dirt until the following day when the lush green sod could be replanted over the final resting place of a schoolteacher named Jane.

A celebration of life for Jane had been held earlier that day in a full school auditorium, where she had taught for many years. The anecdotes shared spoke of a woman of remarkable generosity of spirit who always came forward when anyone needed help of any kind. Her family took turns to describe her as someone who somehow always found the time to help others: volunteering for charities, baking apple pies for the annual bake sale, and countless other gestures that were her way of contributing to a greater good.

Her children told how she took such wonderful care of her elderly parents as they neared the end of their lives and how they could always hear her cheering them on at soccer or Little League games. Babysitting her young grandchildren, she never failed to take an opportunity to teach them the alphabet or read to them before bed. Her husband added how she barely had time for herself.

But now, she had run out of time. What was not said or expressed that day was something that none of those nearest to her who had witnessed her decline over the last decade had wanted to talk about. "What an injustice that someone who was such a good person could die such a horrible, lingering death." She was only sixty-seven years old. Maybe her biggest flaw was that she cared much more about others than she evidently did about herself. Maybe she could have better fought off the cancer if she had taken more time for herself over the years to relax, to recharge, and to be more self-indulgent. It was these relationships in her life and helping others in her community that gave her a calling and a purpose.

She never gave a foothold to the depression, anxiety, or burnout that affected so many of her friends and colleagues. But by no means was she a saint. She could be quite short-tempered and impatient when things did not go her way. Her disappointment when people behaved badly, whether in her direct proximity or far removed in the news, could strike with quick anger. People around her might judge her as spilling over into self-righteousness. But more often than not, she proved to be on point.

The mourners thought about all the wonderful memories they had of Jane that were now tainted with their anger about her stolen future. It was saddening to consider the loss of the twenty-plus years she might have lived. Many of those who watched her in her final months wondered if they, too, would have the strength of character that she exhibited, how she hung in there and persevered without burdening others with her pain and suffering. As her health was clearly failing, she had continued to put the feelings of others first.

Two thousand miles away on another coast, a celebration of a different kind took place a few days afterward—a retirement party honoring the four-decade-long career of Neal, a senior corporate executive. He had worked with great dedication and pride for one of the most trusted American consumer health care product companies. It would be hard to find one household in all fifty states that didn't have at least one of their products in a bathroom drawer or medicine chest, and Neal had played a big role in fostering that appeal.

At the country club, colleagues and coworkers had no loss of words. Everyone had a Neal story to tell, some more long-winded than others. They shared how he had started with the company fresh out of college as a production engineer. But rather than being a nerdy, pocket protector kind of guy, Neal had personality. The portrait they painted of him was how he grew to become a model corporate executive—loyal, responsible, good at what he did, and fun to be around. People in higher places took a liking to him, greasing his way up the corporate ladder.

His career was now coming to a close. *And a good thing at that*, he thought on his way home after the event. The town car he and his wife sat in breezed past the green parkways to their beautiful home. The culture had shifted, and all the standards and norms that he thought were sacrosanct both within his company and the industry had been dispensed with, thrown out like sour-tasting leftovers from a day or two before. And there were all the endless lawsuits.

As the car pulled into the driveway, he grumbled, "Everybody is only into it for themselves." He preferred the company of the faithful dog waiting for him at the front door more than what he had just left.

The old order of things had faded, in some ways for the better, and for others much worse. Both Jane and the slightly older Neal had been children of a resilient generation who had persevered through the Great Depression and World War II. They had been children of the 1950s, formative years of optimism and growth. As the space industry began in the next decade, there was a sense that America and its industry could accomplish nearly anything it set its mind to do. There was a faith and a trust in American ingenuity and the products it produced. Life was good.

Those in the growing, predominantly white middle class enjoyed the fruits of prosperity. A family could generally live well with the paycheck from one wage earner. Thanks to more affordable automobiles, they moved to the suburbs. They traveled farther on vacations with greater ease, thanks to the new Interstate Highway System. Fast food came into being to meet the accelerated pace of life. Nuclear power came online, touted as a boundless source of clean, cheap energy.

There were few voices of dissent to cast doubt about this great progress. Questioning authority was not encouraged. People toed the line. Bottles of formula were fed to infants instead of breast milk. DDT was sprayed on the walls of baby's nursery to kill mosquitos. And closer to home, to Neal's company, baby powder made of talc had been a trusted staple in family life for generations.

Cracks in this myth began to slowly appear. In 1962, Rachel Carson published her groundbreaking exposé, *Silent Spring*, a major catalyst in launching the environmental movement. It talked about how populations of bald eagles were decimated as their eggshells became too fragile to yield offspring. Soon, the insecticide DDT was banned worldwide.

DDT was just one example of the multitude of man-made chemical compounds numbering in the thousands entering into our foods, our water, our medicines, and just about every manufactured product. The beneficial promise and lucrative returns from many of the chemicals spurred a rush to market, sometimes with little or no testing, and perhaps with equipment, methods, and technology not yet sophisticated enough to detect potential issues. Little, if any, thought was given to whether problems from daily exposure might occur many years down the line. Simultaneously, businesses realized they needed more sophisticated information control. More and more corporations wanted to take better control of their messaging, doing their own thinly veiled research and, if necessary, doctoring their findings to rosier outcomes.

The company where Neal started in 1968 was a classic American success story that was mirrored in the histories of so many of the corporations that make up the modern Fortune 500. As the country emerged from the aftermath of the Civil War and Reconstruction in the last quarter of the nineteenth century, a second industrial revolution took place. The agricultural economy gave further ground to the expanding market for manufactured goods, with more people moving from the countryside to urban areas.

The railroads added newfound capabilities to knit together smaller communities that had previously been more isolated and insular. Other innovations in transportation infrastructure also made it possible to ship products more quickly and efficiently, opening up new markets both domestically and for export. European immigrants and the fields-to-factory influx of African Americans from the South to the cities of the industrial Northeast provided millions of new workers to meet the growing demand by industry.

What many of these corporations that rose to prominence in the late 1880s shared was their entrepreneurial roots. An innovator would catch fire with one product. Fueled by its success, new and complementary items would expand their product offerings, developed both in-house or via mergers and acquisitions.

As the company grew, its physical footprint in its town and region expanded accordingly. And so did its power and influence as an economic, political, and social force. Unions came forward as one safeguard to protect workers against this growing power. It would always come down to finding a balance between keeping the production machinery going and giving enough incentive to satisfy employees.

Just as Neal had done, employees would endeavor to stay put at the company for the duration of their careers, instead of the modern-day practice of job hopping for better opportunities and compiling multipaged résumés. Loyalty to the company and the brand was prized and rewarded. There were promotions and raises in salary. There was the promise of economic security in retirement with a good pension.

But just as important was the comfort of the customary, the stability of the day in, day out routine where everyone knew what was expected of them. The small perks also added up, like paid meals, travel, and expense accounts. Management fostered an atmosphere to make the company feel like one large extended family.

There was a price of entry to this world that Neal and all those who came before him and after had to pay from the beginning or be weeded out. The mission of the company and the goals and objectives of the brand demanded the highest allegiance. There was a culture of dos and don'ts that dictated how you behaved and interacted on the job, and not the least was adherence to a pecking order to better hold employees accountable.

While our government sets the rule of temporal law and our spiritual traditions promote eternal law, many corporations view themselves as a world apart, with their own set of strict rules and cultures that do everything and all to preserve their profits, power, and standing.

Chapter 2

The naked little infant boy lay on the changing table. Everything was new for Jane, learning on the job. She wished at times that she had a third arm to manage everything. Two safety pins stood safely nearby to secure the corners of the cloth diaper, along with a waterproof cover. Her mother's occasional help made this new responsibility feel a little less overwhelming with each passing day.

While she wiped him down with a washcloth, she carefully inspected his groin and butt crack for any signs of a rash. She grabbed the baby powder for the final touch before diapering. The subtle perfume of the baby powder awakened one of her earliest memories of her younger siblings. That smell also gave off a feeling of continuity; while the rest of the world might be in chaos, at least that age-old fragrance in the air was an oddly comforting constant.

Adventures in childrearing balanced with her new career as a teacher made for an exciting time for Jane. As much as the late 1960s was a turbulent, violent, and often tragic time in America, there was an abiding hope for the future. Jane held that future in her arms at home with her baby and also with the young children in her classroom (where she would return in a few weeks after maternity leave). Despite the war in Vietnam and the storm of social, racial, and political unrest, Jane had unwavering faith in the power of good. There was no welcome mat in her world for cynicism, pessimism, or defeatism. She was an idealist at heart, and nothing in her life experience so far had done anything to dampen it. She believed in all of her heart that any evil could be uprooted if people with good intentions found a way to team up and work together. Others might scoff at her as blatantly naïve. It wasn't a choice or some belief system imposed on her. It was something she viewed as her nature, an involuntary path.

Jane acted out her vision of a better world as her own experiment into the ripple effect. Even as a young girl, she had discovered how good she felt when she made even the smallest gestures of generosity to help friends, family, or neighbors. She could sense, without necessarily being totally conscious of it at the time, how these interactions changed the energy of the recipients. They became more cheerful and positive and less fearful or protective. Grumpy neighbors would smile, greeting her as she rode past on her bike. Gratitude, she thought, was a surefire gateway to love. All we need is love, as the Beatles pointed out, and Jane saw the proof of that in action. Beginning college, she considered becoming a nurse, a natural choice for one with such a strong caregiver spirit. But second thoughts about being around sickness and disease and feeling powerless at times to help the incurable made the idea of teaching a more palatable option.

It was easy to think that Jane's life was some idealized fantasy of her own making, fueled by the expansive free spirit of the time, pulsating with a soundtrack of music on the AM radio that celebrated being young and alive in the California sun. Maybe her mind resided in a carefree bubble of kindness detached from the heavy burden of victimhood that most people retreated to in more stressful circumstances. But it was hardly an escape from reality. If anything, Jane realized that in her small ways, she could be an agent for positive change.

Working in the classroom, she realized how real change happened one person at a time and how the tiniest acts of goodness toward another could have life-changing impact. She loved the personal interaction with her students beyond teaching. They opened up about their families and daily predicaments that they rarely shared with anyone else. And Jane would help them if she could, with kind words and suggestions.

During this same time, Neal's career path took an unexpected turn. His boss had called him into his office to discuss a new project that was of utmost importance to the company. Up to that point, he had what was considered one of the best jobs in the company. When a new product was developed in their laboratories or acquired from an outside source, Neal was a senior member of the team to take it from prototype through all the stages of development to integrate it into their machinery and ramp it up to full production. Sometimes he felt like he was conducting a symphony orchestra, getting so many moving parts to work in unison and harmony. There was a beauty to the process, and it was anything but routine and mundane. His creative mind thrived on the unique challenges that each new project presented. There were vast opportunities for innovation that were encouraged and rewarded handsomely. If Neal found a way to shave off a half cent in raw materials costs or came up with an adjustment to make the production run more efficiently, the domino effect in profits for the company would be in the millions. This is what built careers and personal wealth portfolios. Christmas was looked forward to and celebrated for extra reason because annual bonuses were given out.

But all of that was about to change. His boss sugarcoated the information about the shift in his duties with enthusiasm and compliments, pumping up Neal the best he could on how he was the perfect person for the job and how the company needed him for this crucial assignment. Neal listened to it all crestfallen. It was as though he had been a rock star selling out arenas and was told that he was now going to be playing the piano bar at the Holiday Inn.

Neal was informed that he was being entrusted as the custodian of the company's most sacred product. Mention the company name in a word-association game, whether in the 1920s or the 2020s, and it would yield the same response: "baby powder." It was the personality of the overall brand—family friendly, a fixture in the medicine chests of every household since the 1890s. It had the trademark scent that Jane and millions like her associated with motherhood, baby, and cleanliness. Although it represented only a single digit worth in profit share for the company, it was as precious as Mickey Mouse has been to Disney. You don't mess with Mickey Mouse. The same applied to the white powder.

At the close of receiving his new directives, Neal was given a thick folder with everything he needed to know about the history and development of the product, including ingredient formulas, raw product sourcing, manufacturing issues, marketing and consumer relations, and distribution channels. The boss asked him to pay particular attention to the last tab in the presentation labeled "Opportunities and Challenges" and marked restricted and confidential.

As he got further into the dossier, Neal got quickly beyond his negative first impressions. It was a far richer field than he had imagined, with baby powder being only the tip of the iceberg in a vast array of commercial and industrial uses of its main ingredient, talc. The soft mineral compound made up principally of magnesium, silica, and water, plus a range of substances in lesser quantities, had been in continuous use, dating back to ancient civilizations. Native Americans made bowls, pots, cooking stoves, and other utensils from it. The Assyrians used it in the form of soapstone to carve cylindrical seals and signets to print impressions into wet clay tiles, while the Egyptians made scarabs and amulets from it. Five thousand years ago, the people of ancient Egypt and Northern India used it to lighten their skin, the first known reference of it as a cosmetic ingredient.

What made talc so valuable stretched far beyond cosmetics. The white stuff on a stick of chewing gum is talc; it prevents it from sticking to its wrapper. The piece of paper you hold in your hands would look much differently without talc. It fills in the space between the cellulose fibers to make it less transparent, whiter, and a better medium for application of ink. Talc can also be found all over our homes in the walls and floors. In paints, it functions as a filler to help the liquid adhere to the wall better and forms a barrier effect against water and corrosive agents, eliminating bubbles, cracking, peeling, and weather-related damage. (This use has been reduced in more recent times since latex paints have largely overtaken oil-based products).

Many of the same benefits apply to its use in sheetrock, caulking, wallboard joint compounds, vinyl flooring and siding, and roof shingles. The food we eat may also contain traces of talc as a chemical carrier for herbicides and pesticides as well as a fruit-dusting agent. Ceramic products are also easier to manufacture and more durable thanks to the magnesium oxide derived from talc. The overview pointed out a long list of attributes that made this compound so valuable and versatile: chemical inertness, fragrance retention, high dielectric strength, high thermal conductivity, low electrical conductivity, luster, moisture content, oil and grease absorption, purity, softness, and whiteness.

Obviously, the company's only interest in the mineral was its applications to the human body, specifically on contact with the skin. Ground into fine powder, talc has been regarded as the perfect ingredient for many cosmetic products because of its many problem-solving properties. Best known is its ability to absorb oils and perspiration produced by the skin. Another plus is how it readily adheres to the skin but also washes off easily. There was no concern about abrasion with regular use because of its inherent softness.

Reading between the lines, Neal understood why baby powder was not just for babies. It was also a staple of locker rooms everywhere, from the YMCA to the fancier country clubs as shower room amenities. The containers of the white powder stood on the shelf under the mirror beside the greenish-blue jars of combs in disinfectant and the cans of shaving creams, plus other assorted aftershaves, hair creams, and tonics. Neal's generation subconsciously associated the fragrances of the powders and lotions with activities they looked forward to, like playing golf or tennis, a welcome respite from responsibility.

A seed was planted in his mind. He thought once he got his feet wet with the division, perhaps he could put his old brand-development expertise to work developing new products targeted to more specific adult demographics. Women were by far the biggest consumers, so why not develop a greater variety of offerings, especially for after-shower deodorants and female hygiene?

The majority of the talc the company used, Neal read on, was dug out of the earth in open pits, the bulk of which was sourced from the metamorphic rocks of the eastern side of the Appalachian Mountains in Vermont, as well as another mine in Italy. It is commonly found in what is called convergent plate boundaries, what usually happens when two different plates push up against each other, forming mountains. Neal had a technical dictionary in reach, as many of these terms were new to him. The report detailed how these deposits formed from the interaction between dolomitic marble and heated waters rich in dissolved magnesium and silica.

Mining talc was a precision operation, done with great caution to avoid contamination with other rock materials, especially ones that would cause discoloration. Drilled, blasted, and partially crushed in the mining process, the talc was sent to a mill for further refining to meet the company's high standards for particle size, purity, whiteness, and other qualities.

Neal went painstakingly slowly through the dossier, working his way to the restricted-access portion toward the end. Each document was there for a reason, and he did not want to skip too quickly through something that might be crucial background for what was to come. He needed to get up to speed as quickly as possible.

As he dove deeply into the restricted material, Neal had been around the block enough times to realize that no situation was ever perfect. There were always trade secrets to safeguard. On the grand economy of scale, you had to be realistic about these things. There were ever-present liabilities that gave opportunities for lawsuits, sometimes for the most frivolous of reasons. These were manageable if kept to a minimum. The court of public opinion would always weigh the benefits of using a product versus the risks. What was different here was a sense of hypervigilance, since talcum powder was an indelible part of the company's wholesome image.

So, the folder was an attempt to prepare for worst-case scenarios, to ideally be ahead of the curve by two or three steps if possible. Where there were flashpoints or vulnerabilities in the days, months, or years ahead, the folder stood ready and prepared. The company should never be caught off guard.

Days quickly turned into weeks and months into years as Neal settled into his position and received plaudits from the company for his innovation and performance, especially for the growing of several new brands that had talc as the main draw.

By the mid 1970s, the restricted-access folder grew in size. The most recent additions reflected the growing concern of health issues related to asbestos. There were reports dating back to the 1890s identifying probable asbestos contamination of raw talc that had been kept under the radar and not flagged as a major public health concern. A form of magnesium silicate, asbestos is a fibrous mineral that is found in the earth's crust. Its use by human beings goes back thousands of years. The embalmed bodies of Egyptian pharaohs were wrapped in asbestos cloth to prevent deterioration as early as 2000–3000 BC. With the advent of the industrial age, asbestos found broad application to a host of products because of its high tensile strength, thermal resistance, low conductivity, and resistance to most chemicals. Almost everywhere you looked, you could find asbestos—in the brakes of your car, in the heating ducts of your home or place of work, wall insulation, hair dryers and toasters, floor tiles, and the list goes on.

The fact that the file was growing was a consequence of society's increasing awareness of asbestos as a serious disease-causing agent. But truth be known, it should have hardly come as a surprise to anyone at the company, even decades before Neal joined it. The contamination of the talc and talc products was first reported in the scientific literature in the 1940s. There was awareness at the time that the presence of asbestos in talc indicated that its use could not be considered to be 100 percent safe. Yet 100 percent safe was exactly what the company promoted, contrary to what they knew to be true.

There was an understanding in the reports Neal read that it just wasn't considered to be a problem. One thing that helped the company maintain the image of product purity was the hardcore fact that asbestos-related diseases like mesothelioma can take decades to develop into deadly cancer. As long as people had shorter life spans or had higher-risk lifestyle factors like heavy smoking, they would more likely die earlier from quicker onset causes.

Neal was smart enough to realize that this little lie about being 100 percent safe was a ticking time bomb. In masking this evidence, the company was burying its head in the sand, wishing against hope that the issue would simply vanish. If the problem received little attention and the cases seemed few and far between, it would be easy for the whole matter to escape under the radar. Given the long-term exposure people have to a range of toxic substances (including asbestos from multiple other sources), lawyers could make it hard to prove beyond a reasonable doubt that baby powder alone was the culprit. The company could also bank on the trust and goodwill they had built over nearly a century.

What was not in Neal's folder was the naked truth that talc, even without asbestos, was never considered safe. Exposure to high concentrations of talc causes an inflammatory reaction in tissues that can be eventually fatal, particularly if inhaled into the lungs. Known as granulomatous disease, this was especially noted in miners and others in concentrated daily exposure in industrial manufacturing. Borne out in later research, much of the disease (in the form of tumors or fibrosis) in this group took as long as ten or twenty years to develop—but much quicker in some cases for those who were also smokers. Often, they would be suffering from lung fibrosis, making the lung tissues so rigid that they could not expand or efficiently exchange oxygen for carbon dioxide. Later, they would develop lung and pleural cancers.

The paper trail assembled by the company was definitive in its defense of its rejection of any responsibility, should a claim arise sooner or later. Neal earmarked two memos in particular:

> The talc used in the company's baby powder is obtained from a selected mine in Vermont where the ore consists of platy and fibrous talc, with only trace amounts of fibrous material (anthophyllite, which has an unusually high iron content and tremolite). It is free of chrysotile fibers, the most commonly used asbestos, which may be called "pure asbestos" by the layman.

Written by a company publicist, the report cited three different research studies by academic institutions as the basis of these findings. The second memo that sparked Neal's attention was similar in that it was hardly the epitome of trustworthy, independent research findings. Drafted by the mine's director of research and development, it spun a rosy picture of a six-month study on its Vermont mine:

> In conclusion, it can be stated with a greater than 99.9 percent certainty that ores and minerals produced from the ores at all Windsor Mineral locations are free from asbestos or asbestiform materials.

Chapter 3

A visit to the gynecologist for her annual exam was high up on Jane's list of her least favorite things to do. No one likes going to the doctor, but all the discomfort, embarrassment, and indignity of being examined with feet in the stirrups was in a league of its own for her. For extra measure, she doused herself with her deodorant powder in the faculty bathroom before driving there for her late-afternoon appointment.

She felt there was one thing that her husband, Phil, would never understand about women in general and herself more specifically. There was nothing in his physiology that was as complicated and domineering as the female reproductive system. After three pregnancies, the roller-coaster ride of hundreds of menstrual cycles, the occasional ovarian cyst, and other assorted pains and unpleasantries, Jane intimately knew this part of her body miles better than any other. "Phil doesn't have to carry tampons in his wallet," she mused. Although he was a compassionate person, her hot flashes in her premenopausal years were hard for him to comprehend as anything more than an occasional annoyance.

As the breast exam was completed, she lay down on the examination chair. Jane remembered the terror of going for her first exam and was thankful that it wasn't as much of a big deal as it was back then. A male physician like Dr. Fisher bending down and probing her always sparked a sense of dread. But the bother of switching to a female doctor was more than balanced by a feeling of trust and safety developed over the years.

Jane also tried to make it through the appointment with as little small talk as possible. Even if it were only a matter of a few extra seconds, unnecessary conversation would prolong the appointment longer than it had to be. When Dr. Fisher asked her how she was doing and if there had been any changes since their last exam, she was similarly reserved. "Everything is fine," she reported.

After he scraped her cervix for the pap smear, Dr. Fisher inserted his gloved fingers farther inside her. As he reached farther in to feel around her left ovary, Jane couldn't help noticing that he was taking longer than she remembered from past pelvic exams. *It's good that he's so thorough*, she thought, while she also felt her body tense up. It sparked a slight hot flash, and her stomach felt tight and a little nauseous.

As he finished the examination, Dr. Fisher told Jane that one of her ovaries felt a little abnormal to him. He suggested doing a transvaginal ultrasound to get a little more detailed information to see if there was anything to be concerned about. A few minutes later, a technician rolled in the portable machine.

As she put her clothes back on to meet with Dr. Fisher in his office, Jane's mind was racing a mile a minute. She thought about all of her friends and colleagues who had been through this mill, confronting what might be their worst fears. If it was just a regular ovarian cyst, he probably would have been quick to say it was nothing to worry about. But looking at all the fancy degrees on the wall and the beautiful, happy pictures of his family staring back at her, she felt that her life had been so fortuitous up to this point. She had been relatively carefree. But as she sat there, she had a sinking feeling in her gut that perhaps the days of taking all that for granted might be slipping away.

Moments later, she walked out of the office in a shock-induced haze. She pressed the button to the elevator and got into her car in the parking lot as if on automatic pilot. The phrases he had just told her played in a loop in her head over and over. "Nothing is confirmed yet, but I suspect ..." "If so, your prognosis is excellent; you'll be fine because we're catching this so early ..." "We'll get you in right away for a CT scan ..." "Before you go, let's draw some blood for some labs ..."

No matter how optimistic Dr. Fisher sounded, cancer (if she had it) was still cancer. Death or the possibility of dying was no longer hypothetical and something that happened to others. It wasn't that Jane was laboring under some grand illusion that she was going to live forever. Rather, she was just so preoccupied with the full spectrum of living that it didn't leave much space for the contemplation of her impermanence. She appreciated the mundane adventures, the responsibilities with the school and with the causes and activism she supported. She cherished the time with her grandchildren, paying forward the way her late mother had helped out with her children. She enjoyed the evening hours with Phil, a cooked meal, a better-than-average wine, and a conversation about everything or nothing. Above all, she appreciated the fleeting moments of peace and quiet, to pause and take the time to let go of everything and just appreciate the beauty of the birds and flowers in her backyard.

As she drove home, she realized that she couldn't wish away what happened at her doctor's office. What concerned her most of all was what to say to her husband and her children. Of course, she would need to avoid alarming them by acting freaked out, even if she was. Instead, she would echo Dr. Fisher's optimism, how even if the worst scenario was confirmed, her prognosis was favorable. She would tell her husband as soon as he came home. From there, they would decide the best way to share it with their adult children, perhaps waiting to tell them in person.

Phil was a bottom-line kind of person, so his response to the news was no surprise to Jane. His immediate responsibility, as he listened to her explain what happened at the doctor's office, was to not to layer on any extra emotion from his side that might add to Jane's burden. He thought it was time for all of her caregiving energy to be directed toward herself.

Inside, however, was another matter. There was a lump stuck in his throat. Well-meaning words were coming out of his mouth, but his thoughts were far distant. The fantasy of walking hand in hand with the lapping waves cooling their feet on the warm beach in the fading rays of the sunset was suddenly supplanted with the nightmare of hanging out at a hospital bed. Maybe this was just a scare, but nonetheless, it would certainly not be the last one.

No use getting too worked up for the moment, he told himself. They would know better in the coming days.

The two-day wait for the appointment for the MRI was interminable, but bright and early, they sat in the waiting room for her name to be called. Jane was shown to a small changing room to put on a hospital gown. A few minutes later, she was asked to lie down on a sheeted bed. Seconds later, the technician pushed a button to load the bed into the imaging tube. The tech was well rehearsed with a calm, reassuring tone, explaining step-by-step what was going to happen.

Claustrophobia was the common side effect of being trapped in a coffin-like tube for minutes that seemed like hours, even though it was open at either end. There were earphones with soothing music and even sedatives available if needed, if she felt uncomfortable with the procedure, but none of it was needed in her case. Jane's anxiety about what they might discover that day was far greater than any discomfort she had in the moment.

It was easy under this stress for her mind to dwell on negative thoughts of doubt and denial as the machine whirled and spun around her. If she was in pain or had even the mildest symptoms of a disorder, this would all be more believable. But she felt perfectly fine. Her irrational mind wanted to believe that they could have it all wrong. But she was a mature adult who knew all too well the ways of the world.

As Jane and Phil walked into his office an hour or so after the MRI was completed, Dr. Fisher fell back on a script he had used hundreds of times. There was a lot of room for improvisation, tailored to his knowledge of the patients and their personalities. There was not a lot of instruction given to bedside manner when he was in medical school. Many doctors were miserable at expressing compassion with sincerity. Getting accepted and surviving medical school required a laser-sharp mind and photographic memory, skills that were highly prized and rewarded. To sit eyeball to eyeball with patients and their loved ones and deliver news with empathy was hardly taught, and maybe it couldn't be. An attentive listener, an effective communicator and emotionally intelligent—you either had it, or you didn't.

Dr. Fisher decided to play it down the middle. These were highly educated, grown-up people and more enlightened than the average. *Tell it like it is and do not embellish*, he thought. *But keep it positive whenever possible.*

It was not encouraging news. The MRI revealed all the markings of the disease. He told them there were other diagnostic procedures to consider. A biopsy would give definitive word on malignancy—a small incision in the abdomen and a tiny tissue sample. They could also take a look at the area for any other troubling signs. If necessary, a PET scan could give more proof if it had metastasized to surrounding tissues and organs. With those results, it would then be possible to stage it and thereby determine the treatment moving forward. He brought up the strong likelihood of a routine hysterectomy, radiation, and chemotherapy. He felt it best to frontload this information. If it didn't pan out that those procedures were needed, Jane would be relieved and grateful. By not deferring it for later, he risked subjecting her to more trauma.

Jane listened without much outward emotional display while Dr. Fisher explained the facts. Over the forty-eight hours she had had to wait since her last visit, she had buttressed herself. Nor was any display of emotional fragility her style. She summoned her strength, thinking of the times she had been wearing the other shoe, helping her students navigate through tragedy and chaos equally as devastating as what she was going through right now.

There was a weird sensation of relief in knowing once and for all what she was possibly facing, Jane couldn't help noticing. Sometimes the anticipation, mind games, and guess work are worse than the reality. One other tidbit that Dr. Fisher mentioned, while leafing through the file in his hands, was the results of her bloodwork. As far as the science could tell them at the time, there were no genetic markers for ovarian cancer that they could find. In that same file, there was no previous mention of any family member or recent ancestor with the disease, something he verified with her again. Idiopathic, meaning "relating to or denoting any disease or condition that arises spontaneously or for which the cause is unknown," was a new and unwelcome addition to her vocabulary.

The main caution Dr. Fisher advised was to move swiftly. It appeared that the tumor was quite small, which was the good news, he emphasized. But ovarian cancer was also fast growing, and needless delay would not work in her favor. Before Jane and Phil left his office, the nurse made some quick phone calls and scheduled the biopsy at the hospital for the next morning.

The surgeon made the first of two small incisions in Jane's lower abdomen. It was termed a "less invasive procedure." She was comforted by the fact it was outpatient (barring complications) and that she would be home later that afternoon. At discharge later that day, she would be given a dozen tablets of an opioid-laced Tylenol called Percocet to have on standby if needed. No matter what the findings would be, Jane entered the hospital that morning at least knowing that she would not suffer the torture of speculating on the wide range of possibilities and uncertainties for much longer. A treatment plan (if necessary) for the next few months would be determined from the biopsy.

The surgeon inserted the laparoscope into one of the holes. The thin tube had a miniscule camera on its end and a small light to illuminate the area of focus for display on the video monitor. The camera also would provide a glimpse at the surrounding organs and tissues to look for any obvious sign of abnormalities or spread. The second incision was made to assist the removal of the ovarian tumor for the biopsy, which would be then sent off to the pathologist for analysis and potential staging.

Two days later, Jane was back at the same hospital in the same surgical suite. The same incision points were to be reopened, with another one added for good measure. The doctor had called her early the next morning after the biopsy with the pathology results. How bizarre it was, she thought, that she had already braced herself for the worst-case scenario as a clever self-preservation scheme. All the worry and upset she had felt since first learning of the problem had already put her through horrific mood swings. But Jane was savvy and self-aware to the degree that she understood that depression was a normal and strangely healthy response to the profound loss she was beginning to experience.

First to go by the boards was the illusion that her body was a perfect machine that would work like clockwork indefinitely as long as she made healthy choices. Gone was the illusion that she could keep on trucking through life in the driver's seat. The assumption that she could keep an appointment she made in her calendar for the next week, the next month, or the next year was no longer a given. And as she learned from the pathology report, gone would also be the physical structure of her womanhood. The uterus and ovaries that had been such a blessing and a curse throughout most of her life would soon become medical waste.

So, depression allowed Jane to hit the pause button, to acknowledge all the mini deaths of things that she had so prioritized, and to give her the space to contemplate what could be the main event of dying itself. Of course, she didn't know with any degree of certainty that this episode could lead to a fatal outcome, and she desired to do all that made sense to delay that onset and restore her health and vitality.

It could feel a little self-indulgent to be in this funk. Shutting out the demands of the world around her during her surgeries and the immediate aftermath had its benefits. It gave her reprieve from taking on the emotional burdens of others, as was her practice. She didn't concern herself as much as she normally would with how her husband was coping with the situation or how disturbed her children might be, seeing her in this state. She became friends with her depression as opposed to fighting the discomfort and malaise or judging herself harshly for being in a state that most people saw as a weakness or a flaw.

The depression acted as a numbing agent against the magnitude of this mutilation. There just wasn't the usual reserve of psychic energy to weather this. Instead, she was stuck comfortably in the emotional basement, with no desire or initiative to lift herself out. Again, she chose not to fight against something she regarded as normal under the circumstances. She would be left alone for the next month, to rest and restore and get ready for the next phase of the treatment protocol.

The oncologist told her that she was in stage 3, meaning there was some concern and precaution to take to fend off spread of the cancer to adjacent tissues and organs. The doctor prefaced it all by saying that they thought they got it all. Once she was healed from the hysterectomy, they would follow up with radiation and chemotherapy.

Hearing this news was strangely reassuring. Her case was routine, everyone told her. They had caught it early. She was going to be all right, they believed wholeheartedly. Her team did this every day for a living. They respected her intelligence and her maturity enough to give her the straight dope if something wasn't right. And most importantly, no one asked if she had her estate planning in order. Although, after smiling at that thought, Jane made a mental note to do it anyway, since it would be negligent in general to put the decision-making burden on her husband

and children, and worse still, have them argue over matters after her passing that could be eliminated with a few strokes on her keyboard.

There was some relief knowing what the immediate future held for her. Over the next four weeks, her energy and her freedom of movement became a little better day by day. She had only needed to take four Percocet in the hours immediately following her surgery once the anesthesia had completely worn off.

As she put the leftover painkillers in a drawer cluttered full of other old pharmaceuticals (some well beyond their expiration dates), Jane began to ponder something she had never given serious thought to before. Never, not once, even at her lowest moments, did she ever think about suicide. But that option suddenly crossed her mind as she put the plastic pill container in a far corner of the drawer. Her mind flashed to the few times she had to have a beloved pet euthanized. They did everything they could to keep their dogs and cats well and with good quality of life. But there came a time when it was the most humane thing to do to end the needless suffering. Why should it be any different for her? she wondered. Now was not the time.

Swallowing a handful of pills was only a consideration but a comforting one to have. It was always good to have choices, she reckoned. Cancer was cancer after all. Her body might lick it this time, but for how long? Maybe ten years before, suicide would have been judged a radical, immoral, and desperate act. But not any longer. The sin, shame, and taboo were not what they used to be. Instead, there was growing recognition of the horror stories of people who hung on too long. She had told Phil that under no circumstances did she want to become a cash cow for the assisted-living facilities. Most wait too long and become too far gone and unable to make life-support decisions, thus prolonging horrible suffering for themselves. She made sure to convey her wishes and give Phil full permission to pull the plug if needed.

Jane's slowly restored sense of well-being took a predictable nosedive as the round of treatments began. The protocol called first for five weeks of radiation, followed by six months of chemotherapy. A few weeks into the radiation, she began to feel abnormally tired, waking up each morning exhausted, as if she hadn't slept a wink. And after each chemotherapy session, she was extremely fatigued and nauseous, so much so that she was not able to go to work, see her friends, or play with her grandchildren. She got her hands on some cannabis, which delivered some relief as promised. Phil told her that he thought she looked really sexy with the bald head, which made her chuckle but didn't discourage her from wearing a wig.

But it was all worth it. A short while after her last chemotherapy session, Jane went in for a PET scan. The oncologist told her that they could find no evidence of the cancer. It was the first time in nearly nine months that she was able to smile. In a short time, she resumed her normal activities. And slowly but steadily, her hair grew back. A local organization providing support to women with ovarian cancer gladly accepted the donation of her wig.

Chapter 4

Some futurists in the waning days of the 1990s foretold of the new millennium and how people would soon be working jobs that hadn't been invented yet. Such was the accelerated pace of change ushered in by the dawn of all this new technology. In the good old days when Neal first started at the company, a new idea might take many months if not years to move from the drawing board to finished product. Planning for the future could no longer assume a leisurely pace.

Businesses had to become more proactive and not rest on their laurels or past performances, especially given Wall Street's volatility. The aftermath of 9/11, the faint haze of which could be seen from Neal's office window, obliterated any vestiges of stubborn, inefficient modes of doing business anchored in bygone times. Like an aircraft that had redundancies built in as backup systems to prevent cataclysmic failures, companies like Neal's more urgently had to consider worst-case scenarios and have fail-safe plans prepared and ready to implement.

Although his business card innocuously listed his title as vice president / director of strategic planning and development, it was all a cloak for a highly secretive enterprise that was deemed essential to the company's continuing growth, reputation, and future. Neal absolutely loved this part of his job. Most if not all of the bullshit he hated about working with a more limited portfolio of responsibilities had become a thing of the past. No longer was he a slave to the annual sales projections of this brand or subjected to petty infighting.

Neal's new job imbued a kind of power and autonomy that he respected and meted out with careful impunity. If he discovered something with one of their products that needed to be addressed, he did it with a silk glove covering an iron fist. He made it understood with a collaborative spirit that it was nothing personal. It was no one's fault. Times were changing. It had been a seemingly good approach back then. But now everyone would benefit by making some adjustments. He was compassionate about the fact that accepting change from the status quo was hard for most of his colleagues, who preferred the predictability of being locked in their individual hamster wheel of routine. Because he knew this game so well, he didn't need a chainsaw. Rather, he became a cheerleader to inspire the team to work together and celebrate these new innovations that would protect them from becoming outmoded and redundant.

He loved his work because it was far removed from routine. Part of his day, he felt like he was like a detective piecing together clues in the innerworkings of his company to root out misdeeds. The other part he relished had the trappings of being an international secret agent, jetting off to all corners of the world as an intelligence operative, using whatever charm and charisma he had to make friends and influence people. More specifically and less glamorously so, his mission was to spy on market trends and the competitive field and cultivate relationships with scientists, researchers, politicians, and journalists.

The corporate jet took off from the private terminal at the small regional airport not far from Neal's office. As often as he got to use the company jet, Neal still felt like a child in a toy store. It was a perk that never grew old. He understood why some ex–US presidents, when asked what they missed most about their time in power, often put Air Force One at the top of the list. He realized how privileged and spoiled he had become the infrequent times there were scheduling conflicts and he had no choice but to fly commercial. Many times, he would have already reached his destination in the private plane in the hours it took to get to the airport early, go through security, wait in the club lounge, and finally board his seat in first class. And he had lost count of the number of times he made it home late at night the same day to his own bed and had been spared the inconvenience of an unnecessary overnight stay in a hotel.

It was only a forty-five-minute flight, but a plane ride avoided five hours on the turnpikes, expressways, and interstates, the inevitable snarls of navigating through the New York City metropolitan area, and the monotony of the New England countryside, punctuated by exits to charming old pit stop diners and myriad fast-food places.

The extra touches made him feel like he was an aristocrat: a smooth Bloody Mary before boarding, the red carpet on the tarmac leading to the plane, the plush custom interior reminiscent of a posh gentlemen's private club in London, the gourmet meal served by the attractive and attentive private flight attendant, and lastly, the speed of being whisked to an awaiting town car with driver upon arrival. And best of all, no road fatigue, so he could hit the ground running.

The task at hand on this trip was a site visit to the talc mine in Vermont that supplied most of the raw mineral for the company's products. Neal wanted to see and experience firsthand every element of the supply chain, as there were storm clouds of trouble ahead. The industry gossip buzzed of legal claims in the works against a talc-based product from one of their competitors. Neal took such information very seriously. From his experience, there was almost always fire where he smelled smoke. In his experience, rumors panned out to have some semblance of truth about 50 percent of the time. The other half was equally divided between being totally false or highly exaggerated. If it came to nothing, he would still get points for being vigilant.

Neal had some concerns that the paperwork in his old file needed to be updated. If the company's products should come under attack in the near future, he needed something better than decades-old data.

Visiting this mine off a seldom-trafficked road in the Vermont countryside had a bit of a covert feel to it. Neal would have loved to bring one of his underlings along as support staff and to have another trained set of eyes and ears at his disposal. But on a matter as potentially sensitive as this, it was kept tighter to the vest. There would be no paper trail on this excursion. Even the pilot's log would be expunged.

If word got out that the company was even the slightest concerned, the vulnerability might attract a pack of hungry predators. So, to be extra cautious, only those few with the highest security clearance and a well-warranted need-to-know would have any knowledge about this visit before, during, or afterward. On matters so potentially sensitive, paper trails were avoided, as the company knew how documents could be subpoenaed in court cases. They could come back to bite them, especially if they provided evidence that the company might have known about a problem earlier than it had let on or shown intent for damage control.

Arriving at the gates of the mine, the shadowy, mixed forest of conifers and hardwoods gave way to an unexpected burst of sunlight. In the clearing stood a tall industrial edifice towering five stories high, painted bright white, color-matching the powdery product that came from the strip mine just behind it. Beside the big white box stood a handful of equally tall silos and a number of other holding tanks and outbuildings. Within view were giant terraced steps into the Appalachian mountainside, where the talc ore was extracted layer by layer by excavators.

Annual visits and inspections from the client were perfunctory, usually at the midmanagement level, a kind of due diligence to show the flag and kick the tires. Exceptions to that might be if there was a sudden change in operations, usually to showcase increased efficiencies and lower costs and keep the client in the loop.

Neal's visit raised some hackles since it didn't fit the normal criteria. The managers carefully choreographed the visit to make sure that Neal would walk away with higher than satisfactory answers to any questions he might have. All the experts were there, from the mining operations head, the geologist, the mineralogist, the chemist, the product logistics expert, and the head of the independent-testing laboratory hired by the mine.

Talc from this mine, the parent company of which was owned by an international conglomerate, could be found in hundreds of consumer and industrial products. If Neal was coming there to fire them, it would not close the business down, but it would make their lives a lot more complicated.

The arrival had the airs of a military general from headquarters coming to inspect a field base. Neal was greeted and escorted into the foyer and then quickly introduced to the key participants. Formalities completed, he was given a hard hat and a white coat, followed by a quick tour of the facilities.

Within moments of taking their seats around the big conference room table, Neal explained why he was there, not totally forthcoming about his true purpose but just enough to extract the info he needed. The cynic in him was well aware that intentions were strongly motivated around the table to inspire the highest confidence and satisfaction with their product and the jobs they were doing. They were there to tell Neal what they thought he wanted to hear. It would be interesting to see whether or not Neal would play along with their well-crafted and rehearsed answers or if he would go full cross-examining attorney on them, trying to punch holes where he could. The last thing he wanted to do was play the patsy. But there was also a part of him that wanted to check the boxes and return home with adequate documentation to confidently demonstrate that the situation was under control.

Without getting into too many specifics, Neal opened by telling them news that was not news to them. What was in Neal's yellowed file dating back to the 1970s was something they were acutely aware of as well. But he informed them that product safety across the board (especially relating to health) was becoming a front-burner issue in today's world as never before. For generations, his company's talcum powder was branded "pure, safe, and gentle." He wanted to know what everyone was doing to uphold these standards. He told them that the media and the public would not just take their word for it. They wanted evidence. Society was becoming more oriented toward guilty until proven innocent. So, everyone got a few minutes to speak to this issue from their particular perches.

Neal got back into the car fairly satisfied with the data he had received. The yellowed paper could now be replenished by a new stack of fresh content with a sufficient credibility to counter any challenges. The mining manager gave a historic overview, detailing the care taken in the extraction process and improvements in methods and technology that mitigated the possibility of contamination on the front end. The lab scientist projected graphics onto the screen behind him, charting testing results over the last ten years and demonstrating compliance for the raw, unprocessed talc ore with purity standards mandated by an international cosmetics industry called the Cosmetics, Toiletries, and Fragrance Association (CTFA). A flow chart explained step-by-step how a sample moved through their laboratory to show their thoroughness and attention to detail.

The chemist then took over and showed even more elaborate diagrams of how the raw talc went through another mechanical process to enhance its purity, called froth floatation. He explained to Neal how the minerals were put into a soup of chemicals and mixed with air. The desired product would attach itself to the small bubbles and float to the top, while the sludge of impurities would sink to the bottom and be discharged through small openings provided for that purpose. While this technology had been around for more than a century, there had been new advancements and tweaks in recent years that made this process even more sophisticated.

When he wrote up his findings in a report for his select group at the highest levels of the company, Neal was not willing to give it all a blanket endorsement. It was like buying a used car and not taking it to a trusted mechanic for a second opinion. Could the data from the laboratory really be trusted? Did they have an unblemished track record? Were their findings ever tested and found credible in a court of law or by independent scientific review? Why on earth did the mine use only one laboratory and not verify the findings with another facility? Were their methods and technology sufficiently powerful and sensitive enough to reliably measure the most minute quantities? Were the safety standards and testing required for cosmetic use of the product reassuring enough, or wouldn't they be on safer ground to do the kind of peer-reviewed, triple-blind studies required to test new medicines?

A week after submitting his report, Neal was called into an office on the top floor. He was thanked for the thorough and well-executed report on his findings. After careful review, the committee was satisfied beyond a shadow of doubt with the product safety findings and no further action was needed at this time, he was told. The product purity claims were deemed bulletproof. Before leaving, he was reminded to shred all copies of this report, as was customary. Neal did as he was instructed.

Chapter 5

The Air France jetliner touched down at Paris Charles de Gaulle Airport in the early evening local time. It was a trip that had been years in the planning. This was not a normal vacation. It was the fulfillment of a promise, one that had been wishful thinking at the time and had warranted the purchase of refundable tickets. Almost five years to the date when Jane got the good news that there was no trace of the cancer in the PET scan, Phil was making good on the vow that they would take a trip to France to celebrate. There was certainly cause for celebration. Someone diagnosed at stage 3 had only a 40 percent chance of surviving that long.

Arriving in the evening was ideal timing for getting quickly acclimated to the time difference. Rather than packing themselves in like sardines in coach, they had splurged for business-class seats for this special trip, so they were able to get a few hours of comfortable sleep in the air. All they needed to do now was stay up for a couple of hours, maybe find a nice Parisian restaurant open late, and have a glass of wine and a light meal before going to bed.

After slumbering at their quaint hotel, they both awoke at 6:30 a.m. with jet lag, disoriented but eager like playful children to get up and wander the side streets and take in the beautiful city as it was waking up. By 7:00 a.m., the boulangeries had already opened their doors, and the smell of freshly baked croissants and baguettes was impossible to resist. There was still a chill in the late-May morning air, for which they were not suitably dressed, but they insisted on sitting outdoors at one of the small tables on the sidewalk, just to gaze at the passersby and slowly savor the café au lait like it was fine wine.

By 2:00 p.m., they took a taxi to the Gare de Lyon to board the bullet train to Nice. By 8:00 p.m., they would be at their hotel overlooking the beach and the azure-blue Mediterranean. Their itinerary, planned well over a year before, called for them to escape the urban areas and get out to explore the countryside of Provence. They rented a car early the morning of their third day and ascended the windy roads. The city and suburbs gave way more quickly than they imagined to the idyllic villages, farmlands, and orchards. It looked exactly how they had imagined from travel documentaries and from postcards received from friends over the years.

It felt like an enlightened choice as Phil stole a sideways glance at Jane. She took in this landscape with a smile that beamed serenity and gratitude. Back home, their community was literally a disposable thing. Like a beautiful young movie star who grew old and wrinkled, so many buildings that had stood in the Tinseltown of her childhood had been torn down, with no real consideration about preserving history and tradition. She commented to him how these views through the car windows had probably been little altered for decades if not centuries. The walls of the ancient farmhouses were built to last, and the toll of the elements—the rains and winds and the sunbaked heat and winter frost—had only made them more beautiful to behold.

She thought as well about all the generations of families who had lived and labored, broken bread together and made love, and taken their very first and last breaths within the four walls of these ancient dwellings. It took them so much backbreaking effort back then to work the fields and tend the livestock, to get water, to make wine, to weave and sew their clothing, and to care for the young children and the elderly. Everything was done by hand.

Life spans were much shorter back then and only started increasing over the last half century, she reckoned. People were born, they worked, they procreated, and then they died, sometimes only living from age thirty-five to fifty, and maybe if they were lucky, they got to sixty-five or older, but those were the exceptions. Three generations ago, there were no tractors or kitchen appliances, let alone PET scans, chemotherapy, and transcontinental jumbo jets.

When they stopped at a small churchyard in one of the villages, Phil looked at the gravestones and remarked that many younger women buried there had no doubt died in labor. Equally surprising was how many stones there were for infants ranging from newborns to two years. It was an extraordinary place of beauty that was easy to romanticize, but such a hard life they must have had, Jane thought. Hopefully, they were able to find moments to cherish life, just as she was now breathing the sweet air of Provence. Or was she just the self-indulgent lucky one? She had seen many paintings of pastoral landscapes featuring people at work and at play, like the one now outside her car window, in books and art museums. They confirmed to her that life was not all drudgery for these people. Many of those depictions documented the rituals of their lives, at festivals, religious holidays, weddings, barn raisings, and harvests.

Her mind could not help but think about a sadder reality. Had she lived here a half century ago, there would most certainly be a tombstone listing the dates of her birth and her premature death. Her children would have watched as the village doctor did all within the limited measures he could to make her comfortable in her last days. There would never have been any talk of a cure, since nothing of the kind existed back then for the kind of cancer she had. Morphine and other opioids that could have dramatically reduced her pain were hardly commonplace and probably not affordable for those living more isolated in a country village and with meager financial means.

Moreover, she pondered, the people who lived at that time probably had a much different attitude about death than the people of the affluent San Fernando Valley area of Los Angeles at the dawn of the twenty-first century. These villagers were surrounded by death all the time. They slaughtered their pigs, cows, and chickens on a daily basis. Praying over the corpses of their family members and neighbors at wakes was an accepted part of life. With a stronger faith in an afterlife in paradise, perhaps they welcomed death less fearfully.

There was no more room on the itinerary for morbid thoughts. Over the next seven days, Jane and Phil were busy taking in all of the pleasures and delights that Provence had to offer. No matter where they ventured, and regardless of what direction their gaze turned, there was a feast for the senses that fed their bodies, minds, and spirits unlike anywhere in the world they had ever been before. Perhaps what Jane had been through in surviving ovarian cancer made them appreciate the beauty around them in the smallest details: the perfectly balanced arrangement of flowers in a bouquet in the outdoor market, the display of fresh fruits and vegetables in the local shops that seemed infinitely more colorful and fragrant than back home, the boutiques with the distinctive textile designs and sweet incense of lavender soaps, the bleating of young goats playing in a field.

The restaurants where they dined were all extraordinary. Unlike some of the fancy restaurants where they had eaten back home, there was a perfection in the simplicity of the whole experience, down to the smallest details. Nothing was done just to impress. The seating, the menus, the presentation and plating of the food, the unhurried pace that allowed them to savor each morsel, each sip of the wine that made them feel that for a brief moment, everything made sense and all was in harmony.

Everything and everyone working in the cafes and restaurants reflected an authenticity from field to table, a culture and a pride of doing everything to near perfection. Their favorite meal was saved until their last evening. Adorning the walls of La Colombe D'or were nearly century-old paintings and drawings from renowned impressionists who used their works to barter for food and drink from the establishment long before they were rich and famous. Jane basked in the thought of that exchange of arts, the visual for the culinary. The paintings had grown in value, perhaps in the hundreds of thousands if not millions of dollars, but the chance to bask there and take in it all just for a couple of hours was like depositing happiness into her bank account.

For that week in Provence, Jane was in her garden of earthly delights. It didn't matter any longer what hell she had been through with doctors and hospitals in the recent years, the exhaustion and nausea, the dark days when she didn't know if she would ever emerge from the tunnel. She had survived. And she looked at those fragrant days in Provence as a divine dividend of the highest order.

Chapter 6

It was a perfect sunny weekend afternoon in late October. No one appreciated it more than Jane as she played in her backyard with her two youngest grandchildren.

It had been over a year since the vacation in France. The trip had in many respects accentuated what was already present in her. So many who have had a near brush with death often come out of it with a surprisingly more positive attitude about life. As strange as it sounded to her, there were people who willingly exposed themselves to such dangers. It was ridiculous in her mind to hear them talking about the spiritual payoff of squaring off against Mount Everest or rock climbing without ropes or safety gear. Life was precarious enough. Adrenalin was not her drug of choice.

Coming back from a disease like ovarian cancer, survivors often see the second chance of life given to them as bonus time. They have already gone through the mill of understanding and accepting their impermanence. They have a newfound, hard-won perspective. All Jane had to do was think about the other women she had met in the waiting room at the chemo sessions who didn't make it.

Jane realized that splashing in the pool with her granddaughters was a gift that had a similar footprint to her trip to Provence. Being able to cherish and be totally present in this moment was a privilege denied others.

Before the cancer, her mind in that backyard might have been in several places and realms of time at once. With one eye looking out for the kids, she might be sketching out plans for the upcoming work week, wondering if she should buy groceries today or put it off to tomorrow, perhaps perseverating about some unpleasant interaction with an acquaintance the week before.

In contrast, she felt gratitude for living in what could be best described as a state of wakefulness. This expanded consciousness was no longer just a place that she might visit from time to time; it now felt like her default setting, her real home. How easy it had been to achieve that state of mind in the past by going to Provence or hiking in the middle of a beautiful forest, but it could quickly vaporize returning to the drudgery of reality. Situations that had tested her patience and irritants that easily knocked her off center now seemed to have diminished priority in her life. Lying on a reclining lounge near the pool's edge, she could not remember ever being so perfectly still in her mind to simply marvel at a nearby bee pollinating a flower. Similarly, she loved listening to the silly babble of her granddaughters at play, absorbed in their joy of discovery and, at least for now, shielded from the suffering of the human condition.

Less pleasant was her similar hyperawareness about any real or imagined abnormal sensations in her body. Undeniably, she had some variation of PTSD from the whole circus of getting cancer and the trauma of the operations and treatment that followed. A bit of indigestion or the pain of a paper cut were enough to take her away momentarily to an anxious and unhappy place. There were also nagging side effects from all the procedures that were daily reminders of what she had been through. But with the passage of time, they became more annoying than painful. For example, she could swear the skin that had been exposed to the radiation treatment was more sensitive and prone to rashes and inflammation than adjacent areas. She also had to avoid clothing that put pressure on the scar tissue around incisions. It could feel like pins and needles, especially belts and waistbands or fabrics that were stiff and abrasive to the touch.

Sometimes, she would drift off into the fantasy that she was still eighteen years old, as long as she was not within sight of a mirror. Feeling as good as she did while resting and watching her grandchildren, it was easy to project the vitality of youth back on herself. When she would see a beautiful young woman out and about in town, Jane would smile at her, not with schadenfreude but with an appreciation for the transient nature of beauty. *Enjoy it while you can, because it is a cruel reality that you will soon need eyeglasses to read, your breasts will sag, the cellulite in your butt and thighs will multiply, the emerging crow's feet on your face will grow into full-scale wrinkles, and your muscles and ligaments will lose the elasticity and gracefulness you thought would last forever.* It was no different from the flower beside her that would soon drop its petals and shrivel in the darkening autumn chill.

But as she got up from the lawn to chase the children around the garden, Jane left any such illusion behind. She was hardly a ballerina maneuvering herself back on her feet. Her core strength that normally was activated to get up was not an effortless, graceful, fluid movement but a navigation around the aforementioned aches and pains. It was a mixed blessing when their mother came to pick them up later that afternoon.

When she finally got to sit in her favorite chair at the end of the day, she felt a little extra run-down. Maybe she was catching a cold. At one point that afternoon, after some particularly high-octane game chasing the girls, Jane was forced to sit down to catch her breath. This was out of the ordinary but certainly explainable if she was coming down with something.

But no cold or flu ever came in the days that followed. The shortness of breath she felt chasing the girls persisted as her only symptom, and after a week, she made an appointment to see her doctor.

Chapter 7

It was called a retreat, but it was not one of those touchy-feely staff-development workshops that had become in recent vogue. Instead, it was a think tank session to deal with some increasing storm winds in their industry. Held at a palatial Upstate New York manor, the participants were scheduled to meet all afternoon, have a beautifully catered dinner consuming a reasonable amount of fine wine and spirits, overnight in guestrooms and cottages, and then have a morning session until noon before getting an early start to their weekend.

The meeting was called at the behest of Neal. He had been promoted four years earlier to become the head of the company's consumer health division. His responsibilities included overseeing all over-the-counter personal care products for the retail market. It was a lucrative-paying job. Incentives and performance bonuses at his upper-management level were doled out in the form of stock options. If he decided to retire on the spot, that portfolio alone would have supported a life of luxury.

As the assembled group passed around the agenda, Neal asked each of them to introduce themselves and briefly describe their particular areas of expertise. A good portion of the group knew one another well, but new players had come into the fold. Outside consultants and experts with know-how on complex issues had long become the norm, a recognition that the information flow and networking from in-house sources was usually inadequate. Henry Kissinger reportedly once said, "An expert is someone you hire who has already made all the mistakes." Around the table were some highly skilled, battle-tested samurais.

The dark cherrywood-paneled walls and the massive antique conference table were trappings of the power, status, and privilege that built and sustained this imposing manor house. The grandeur of this setting was deliberate in some respects. It was something unspoken that no one wanted to leave the palace for a humbler, less lavish life. There was plenty of personal incentive to do all that was necessary to preserve and protect this kingdom.

Hanging high up on the wall between the taxidermy trophies of hunted animals was a bright white screen on which tables, graphs, and various other illustrations would be projected to imprint the data in visual form. There were also easels with whiteboards, markers, and erasers, along with old-fashioned blank-paper flip charts to spontaneously capture key words and bullet points worth remembering for further consideration.

At the head of the table, chairing the meeting, Neal cut to the chase describing the purpose for the meeting and the objectives that their time together would hopefully produce. Before their leather seats could get warm, the lawyers, doctors, research scientists, and product-safety experts were told in blunt terms that theirs was an industry that was under assault. None of them had been living under a rock. Their only surprise was that the matter had now finally ripened and risen to the level of high alert.

Neal described the current situation to the group, likening it to the analogy that they were all living on an active earthquake fault. The big one could hit any day now, or, conversely, it might just be a tremor. So, what choices did they have? They could move to safer ground. They could ride it out and hope for the best. Or they could proactively reinforce their walls and foundations to better withstand its destructive force.

For years if not decades, there were little secrets that had been skillfully obscured using a playbook of deceit, deception, denial, and deflection. It was understood without stating the obvious, listening to Neal's opening remarks, that nothing was going to radically alter that approach. There was still much to gain by holding steady and not abruptly shifting course.

If anything, Neal wanted concrete ideas on what they could do to start shoring up the walls. It was not too late. Time was still on their side.

The projector heated up quickly as images flashed on the screen, one after the other. The lead scientist provided the narration to the slides, variations on the same theme. It looked like nothing more than sharp splinters of wood and a few asteroid-looking blobs juxtaposed against a textured background of randomly scattered, small crystalline bubbles.

This was all about getting to know the enemy. The images of asbestos fibers in samples of diseased lung tissue captured by a powerful electron microscope were cringeworthy. It didn't take a rocket scientist to envision the damage that these miniscule fibers could wreak. Imagine the disproportionate pain from a tiny splinter in a finger. At least we can remove it with a tweezer and heal from it quite quickly. But these particular fibers stay in our bodies and accumulate over the years without remedy or recourse.

The medical expert took over from there, talking about asbestos in the most clinically neutral manner possible, presenting the generic data to make sure they were all operating from the same set of scientific facts. Much of what they heard was based on substantial and sustained exposure to asbestos in patients who worked in industries that mined, manufactured, or handled the fibers as part of their daily work. These were the cases that made it to court, resulting in big fines or settlements and setting the groundwork for comprehensive environmental regulations.

He went on to talk about what was scientifically proven and what was only speculation about the asbestos and its adverse effects, referring to one peer-reviewed article after another. There were gray areas and ambiguities aplenty that were exactly the kind of material Neal and the attorneys were keen to know about. Neal listened with rapt attention, nodding his head almost on cue, as if to signal to the others that here was an important point to put a star next to. For example, they learned that it could take thirty to forty years of exposure for malignant mesothelioma to develop in a patient. *Toxic initiator chemical* was the term the doctor used to describe the process that locks in the mutation that results in the cancer. Among the cases studied, it was curious why only a small percentage of the workers exposed to the toxin got it, while most did not. Neal interrupted the presentation to ask if there were other family history, lifestyle, or genetic factors that could explain it. Very likely, he was told. Neal nodded approvingly. The attorneys in the room sharpened their pencils on this point as well.

Another expert, a doctor and specialist in industrial hygiene, took over to discuss the current findings regarding talc. Again, it was well known in the cases the previous doctor mentioned how workers mining and processing talc over the years, with minimal or inadequate protective gear, could develop granulomas and fibrosis with exposure to the talc alone, typically in the form of noncancerous tumors and inflammation. The point this expert was making gave credence to the company's claim of product safety because of the far lower exposure levels with normal consumer use. There were also many other sources of exposure to asbestos in the air and in other products. So, it was as much about shifting blame as it was about downplaying the role of their products. Complex mathematical formulas were projected on the screen, calculations for almost any situation imaginable. One such graph charted how long the powder might stay in the air with normal application in relation to the exact dimensions of the bathroom, even factoring in the body size of the user.

Since so many of the company's consumers were women, Neal wanted to hear about any differentials in the numbers on how women were affected versus men. A research scientist whose job it was to monitor scientific journals spoke to the topic. She told the group there was apparently no link between women and the male family members working in high-risk exposures who came down with cancer.

One of the lawyers interrupted. "There has been some mention in some industrial products cases claiming that some women cleaning their father's, husband's or children's clothes also get lung tumors and mesotheliomas. They claim it is termed household or secondary exposure, much like cigarette smoke. What is the data on that?"

The researcher brushed it off. She told the group that there was not sufficient research tracing potential sources of asbestos that could be causing mesothelioma in women. Without corroborating research, those cases would be termed idiopathic, she added.

Neal sat back in his chair. Idiopathic sounded more like "idiotic" in his reckoning. It was like throwing your hands up in the air in resignation. He was not satisfied and wanted bulletproof answers.

Furthermore, Neal wanted to know how the company could be specifically protected against the type of lawsuit against a competitor's talc-based feminine hygiene product that had recently appeared on a California court docket. This was something personal. More than twenty years before, Neal had taken the initiative to move the company into specially targeted products for this then-underserved market. As further niche markets were developed, reaching out to women of color and expanding in international territories, the category had only grown to be more lucrative.

The company's head of research and testing reiterated what was certainly not new information to Neal. The company stood by its claims of product safety that had been substantiated by rigorous testing protocols to the highest standards of the cosmetics industry. Rest assured, he said, they could go into any court of law and present strong and convincing evidence that could successfully allay any concerns about asbestos.

One of the outside attorneys, who had been a well-regarded veteran of the tobacco wars in the 1970s, interrupted to ask a question. He wanted to know if the electron microscope pictures of the asbestos fibers they had been shown earlier were part of the company's approved testing protocol. Yes but only for prescription products that had to go through FDA-required testing standards, the company's research head acknowledged. "Over-the-counter talc products are regarded as cosmetics and exempt," he explained. It was a solid loophole but one of those buried in the fine print that could come back to bite.

Chapter

8

The examination room at her family doctor's office was not larger than a closet. The space felt even smaller than usual, as if the walls were closing in on her. It was easy to feel claustrophobic in such a confined space, given the shortness of breath Jane had been experiencing since that day with her granddaughters in the backyard.

It was easier, thanks to the internet and all the new online resources, to try to be your own doctor. Jane had entered the search terms relating to her symptoms. Checking herself against all the possible causes listed, she concluded it was impossible to come away with any plausible explanation. Shortness of breath was the sign of dozens of various ailments and diseases. Could it be the onset of asthma, a walking pneumonia, or some other inflammation caused by an allergy or an infection? Or was it something more serious and degenerative, one of a dozen or more lung and heart diseases that were the sign of big trouble? The big disclaimer she read on every site was if symptoms persisted over a week, to see a doctor immediately. At least that was a box she could check.

Living in an ozone-ridden, breathing-compromised place like Southern California, she dreaded the idea of being one of those elderly people she would regularly see at the supermarket wearing a nasal cannula and carting behind them a cannister of oxygen. The whole idea of losing her independence and being tethered to some external apparatus just to function was abhorrent. Hopefully, she thought, as she waited for the doctor to knock on the door, he would perhaps put her on a puffer or maybe give her a prescription for an antibiotic and tell her to see him in a week or so.

Once Jane told him why she was there, he immediately listened to her heart and lungs with the stethoscope. He told her that her heart sounded fine, but just to be sure, they did a cardiogram, which also proved to be normal. Looking a little perplexed and a bit unnerved at not seeing anything that could explain her symptom, he asked her to take a deep breath as he once again put the head of the stethoscope more determinately against her chest cavity. Jane told him that she felt a sticking pain in her back when she inhaled that deeply. He asked her to repeat the breaths as he continued to listen.

He took out the earpieces and placed his instrument on an adjacent counter, then paused for a moment to choose his words carefully. It was clear he was not sure what he was dealing with, but it was safe to say her symptoms were for causes not unfounded. There were scratching sounds, he told her, that often indicate pleurisy, an inflammation of the tissues that separate the lungs from the chest wall. He could not do anything more than write out a prescription for a chest x-ray.

When she returned home, Jane immediately called the hospital to get the next available radiology appointment the next day. Her next dilemma was what to tell her husband. The first thing out of his mouth when he got home from work would be to ask how things went at the doctor's and, more specifically, if he gave her any answers about the shortness of breath. More than anything else, she did not want to alarm him. He, too, had emotional scar tissue from her bout with ovarian cancer. She did not want to alarm him and set the roller-coaster ride in motion for what might only be a minor infection. So, she decided to keep it vague and not share with him anything about going in for an x-ray. She scripted out the whole conversation in her mind. "The doctor heard some scratching sounds and thinks I might have some inflammation, pleurisy perhaps."

"So, did he give you some medicine for this?" Jane was a little stumped at how she might answer that.

Being evasive to her husband was not something she did gingerly, especially about something this important. You tell one fib, and then you need to tell a hundred more to cover it up. Sure, she had told him some white lies over the years on some matters to save embarrassment or protect sensitive feelings, but this was different. It felt like she was betraying him. But the price to pay was worth it, she decided. She just did not want to put him through what might be totally unnecessary trauma. If the x-ray results were no big concern, the matter would be put to rest. Another justification was that she did not want to attract all that worrying energy that was too fresh of a reminder of all they had gone through with the last big scare. She hoped the last line in the script would satisfy his concern and put the matter to rest or at least on hold. "He just told me to monitor it and check in with him in a couple more days."

A nurse from her doctor's office called the day after her x-ray was taken. Jane was told she needed to go back to the hospital and get an MRI. She put the phone down and went totally numb. There was no way to mask what was going on. Her husband could almost sense the disturbed energy through the walls of the garage as he was getting out of the car. She told him point-blank that the doctor was sending her for more tests.

Four days later, Jane and Phil drove to her doctor's office with foreboding to discuss the findings from the x-ray and the MRI. Good news travels fast and usually without formality. Bad news requires a sit-down in a doctor's office.

There was something between her lungs and her chest wall, they were told. A biopsy would be needed to know for sure. It was understandable that the first question out of Jane's mouth was blunt and to the point: "Do you think my ovarian cancer is back?" The doctor said he could not say for sure, but it would be highly unusual for it to show up at that site.

Instead, Jane and Phil were peppered with questions as to whether any of them or any member of their families had worked with asbestos. Or did they have hobbies like fixing up cars that might have exposed them, or did they ever do any kind of construction work? Jane replied that she was a teacher and Phil was an accountant, so neither of them, nor their children, had ever been around asbestos to their knowledge.

There were questions Jane would have liked to have asked then and there, but she could tell that her doctor was only willing to go so far in jumping to any conclusions. There were no test results that could shed light with any certainty. He had stated in incontrovertible terms that it would take a biopsy to know for sure what she was facing. As the next step, she was being shuffled off to a pulmonologist.

What made it extra unnerving was the speed at which she got in to see this new doctor. It wasn't a receptionist saying, "The earliest appointment we have is in six weeks." She was rushed in within two days. How comforting it would have been if they said it wasn't urgent and booked her weeks out. There hadn't been time to lose with her ovarian cancer; her memory suddenly flashed with a cold shudder.

If she was looking for any resolution from the pulmonologist, Jane would most certainly have set herself up for another disappointment. Yet another person in a white coat could only tell her that he had suspicions, not unlike her primary care physician had said forty-eight hours before. After doing a breathing test and listening to her heart and lungs, he started asking the very same questions about asbestos, and Jane gave him the same answers in return.

The only way left to get this thing properly diagnosed was to get the biopsy done. The thoracic surgeon took her step by step through the procedure. A few days later, the deed was done, and she was allowed to go home the same day. The surgeon told her before she went home that he would have the results back from the pathologist by the following week.

"You have mesothelioma," the surgeon told Jane and Phil in his office. "It is not a recurrence of your ovarian cancer."

Surprising herself, Jane was remarkably calm hearing this news. After all, it was déjà vu. She already knew what having cancer was like. She knew she had survived it. What she wanted to avoid at all costs was the traumatic and exhausting emotional roller coaster of the first time. She realized that reliving the shock and fear she had when learning she had ovarian cancer was a lot of wasted energy that could have been better saved up for the bigger job of healing. Sometimes the anticipation is far worse than the actual experience.

That peaceful resignation disintegrated almost as quickly as it had manifested in the first place. Wishful thinking can be a fool's game. Mesothelioma, she was told, has no cure. Left alone, she could probably live another twelve months. Removing the tumor, which the surgeon felt confident he could do, would extend her life span for an additional twelve months and in some cases for several more years. But it would grow back, she was told. "They all will eventually come back, and when it does, there is nothing more we can do."

"Isn't there any other form of treatment like radiation or chemotherapy?" Phil asked, trying to inject the smallest ray of hope into the death sentence. They were told that radiation did nothing, and chemo only marginally more, perhaps mitigating some symptoms but not conclusively extending longevity. It could be said that its potential benefits were not worth the toxic side effects.

After asking to talk for a few minutes privately with Phil, Jane agreed to have the surgery.

Chapter 9

The propofol that entered the IV catheter inserted in Jane's hand made her feel like she was being gently wrapped in a warm, silken blanket. The nervousness and tension in her face quickly faded as she drifted off, and all her muscles became slack and servile to the force of gravity. It was at best a brief moment of interlude, the intermission between the onslaught of worry, fear, and torturous anxiety in the days leading up to the surgery—and the anticipation of a slow, exhausting recovery that could take weeks or perhaps months. And given the incurable nature of the cancer, every ache and pain would come to be seen in the prism of a death watch. The questioning would begin about whether it was temporary or a sign of big trouble ahead.

In the days counting down to her surgery, her emotions had swung back and forth like a pendulum. When her mind was peaceful and her body offered no impediment, Jane believed in her heart and soul that she would live each day to her fullest, squeezing out every single droplet of nectar. There were stories of miracles in which people got the last laugh at the death sentences the doctors had given, the triumph of the spirit over the flesh. Jane did not want to harbor any thoughts that might diminish the long shot chance of being one of those miracles. But when the pendulum swung to the other side, she was overwhelmed and overpowered by the existential suffering of it all. Was it worth putting her body through this procedure only to perhaps linger in an inhumanely prolonged and severely compromised state of diminishing?

In her own parents, Jane had seen how her mother transitioned rather swiftly but still with her cognitive abilities intact, very much the bright spirit until the end. Her father went slowly and torturously, as Alzheimer's gradually asphyxiated the man he had once been, leaving only a withering, delusional shell. As she looked at her own predicament, anything remotely resembling her father's story was nothing to repeat, nothing she wanted to put herself or her family through.

"How will I come out of this? Will I be a whole person? Or will I be limited to what I can do? Will I have to have oxygen?" These are the questions that everyone asks their doctor before such a surgery, and Jane was no exception.

Jane had come in to draw blood and urine for her labs and have one last examination a few days before the operation. Her doctor told her that in a worst-case scenario, where they would have to remove one of her lungs, she would still be able to have the trappings of a normal life. She would be able to do normal daily routines, just at a little slower pace. "You may not be able to run after your grandchildren, but you can walk instead."

She then naturally wanted to know what to expect in the immediate aftermath of the surgery. There was no expectation in her mind that this was going to be as easy as her last episode with the hysterectomy. It was all like being at the butcher shop, only she was the slab of meat on the chopping block.

He told her again in the worst case how she would be in intensive care for the first couple of days, sedated, intubated, and on a respirator. Morphine for the first three days, then opioids for a week or two after that for pain control. Then she would be weaned off the drugs and would focus on her healing and adjusting to any reduced breathing capacity.

Her last question did not have such a clear-cut answer. She wanted to know what the chances were that they would have to remove the lung. She knew that the mesothelioma only affected her one side. The other lung and its surrounding tissues were still healthy. But the x-rays, scans, and biopsy were not exhaustive proof for him to give her an absolute answer. There was no other option than to go in and make that determination on the operating table. Jane signed a permission form in case they needed to remove the whole lung or a portion of it.

To begin the operation, the nurses carefully rolled Jane's limp body onto her side to give the surgeon the best access to the chest cavity. He carefully positioned his scalpel on her back from about the sixth rib from the top and guided the blade down the chest, parallel to her spine, curving outward along the contours of the rib cage. The team hovering over the table stood ready with sponges, gauze, and clamps to control the bleeding and keep the area clean and unobstructed.

Once the surgeon removed the pleural lining, he was able to see the extent of the disease, specifically the visible tumor growth. He had done enough of these surgeries to judge very quickly and with good assurance if more radical measures were needed. Unfortunately for Jane, it would not be sufficient to remove the handful of small tumors he found and scrape the area. The cancer growth and spread to the lung tissue was clearly evident. There was no other choice than to remove the lung in its entirety.

As he stitched up the incision, the surgeon was relaxed enough at this point to start bantering with two medical student observers who were hovering in the background. "It's remarkable how long it takes for these tumors to grow. The patient has probably had these for years if not decades, and she was asymptomatic only until recent weeks. But once we do surgery, the timeline changes. Mesothelioma grows much more quickly after surgery."

The nurses packed up and labeled all the tissue samples in bags for delivery to the hospital pathology department. Upon arrival, the tissues would be first coded with an ID accession number linked to the patient, much like the labels put on blood test tubes. They would then be processed into thin slices and stained with colored dyes to identify the cellular features and patterns of cell growth. Looking under the microscope at sections of tissue, the pathologist might add additional coloring agents called immune stains to more specifically identify the relevant structures and types of molecules in the cancer. The readout from the stains would be able to irrefutably confirm the mesothelioma and its type—fibrous, epithelial, or mixed. With the pathologist's report, the doctor could give Jane a more specific read on her prognosis and if she could be a candidate for possible postsurgical chemotherapy that had recently begun to show some efficacy.

The pathologist went one step further to check Jane's sample for asbestos, since it was well established that it is the cause of most mesotheliomas. Since this form of cancer is mostly caused by the asbestos, her tissue sections were observed under the microscope using a third stain that would reveal in blue tint asbestos fibers that commonly become coated in the lungs with iron and protein. A polarizing microscope would be the last step to check for the presence of any uncoated asbestos fibers or other mineral-type materials that could help substantiate the cause of the tumor. As a routine matter of course, the tissue samples would be preserved for an indefinite period into the future in case any further analysis would be needed. Jane would learn the results in the report in the follow-up meeting with her doctor to discuss her prognosis and recommended treatment plan.

Once she was taken off the respirator and weaned off the sedation, she began returning to consciousness or something close to it. She opened her heavy eyelids and saw Phil standing next to her bedside, holding her hand and saying comforting words of reassurance that were heard but not fully comprehended. "I don't want to stay in this hotel any longer," she muttered, barely audibly and in slow motion. "Let's get out of here. When is our train going?" She was obviously hallucinating, Phil surmised, probably dreaming that they were on their trip in France. The attending nurse whispered to him that this state was pretty normal and would pass quickly once the drugs wore off.

Later in the day, Jane was transferred out of intensive care, as she was breathing adequately on her own and was becoming more lucid. Gradually, the nurses would try to get her to sit up and hopefully start walking, a few steps to the bathroom to start. The effort it took was exhausting. It is easy to take for granted the clockwork coordination of muscles needed to do the simplest movements. But when muscle, cartilage, and bone have been severed to such an extreme degree, the mind quickly has to come up with plan B. A sneeze or a laugh can be unbearable. Would the stitches tear and the wounds reopen in contorting to roll onto a side and lift up the upper torso? Such were the fears going through Jane's mind as she struggled in the heat of the moment.

With each successive day in the hospital, there were tiny, incremental improvements in Jane's condition and outlook. She felt less anxious about whether she was getting enough oxygen in the one lung. She took deeper breaths, less fearful that it would burst from the exertion of its doubled workload. The drain in her lower chest had been removed, and she felt less tethered to all the tubes, especially when she got up from her bed to go to the bathroom or for walking therapy. Improvement in her stamina, although still dramatically compromised, was measured in how many extra steps she was able to make going down the corridors. She knew it wasn't cool, but she couldn't help herself as she peered into the open doors and stole glances at her fellow patients. Did they seem worse off than she was? Sometimes she was convinced that they were silently asking the same thing about her.

All she could think about was going home, seeing her children, and watching her grandchildren play. She knew that the morphine and opioids in her system were giving her a temporary stay from the painful reality she was enduring. There was a strong temptation to believe "This was easier than I thought it was going to be," but she was smart enough to know that it was an illusion not to be trusted. There would be hard days of healing ahead. If it was in fact a more horrible recovery period than her ovarian cancer, there would surely be days of tears, anger, and depression to follow. She laughed at the thought that this was like waiting for the impending visit of an intolerable houseguest. Both would only stay for a while and would be gone before long, so best to just go with the flow, the ups and downs, and not waste her precious energy on beating herself up about it.

There were no balloons and colorful welcome-home signs when Jane finally got her wish to go home, nor were they needed. She was just happy to be back in her cozy cave, where she could rotate between the living room sofa and the bedroom and not worry about anything else in the world other than getting better and regaining some semblance of normalcy for however much time she would be granted.

Chapter 10

"How much is enough?" That was the existential question Neal was asking himself on many fronts. He had read a magazine article some years ago detailing the Tibetan Buddhist notion of hell realms. According to the article, it wasn't some destination where people went after their deaths. Instead, it was a place populated with human beings who were very much alive—with one caveat: those hell realms existed solely in their minds. And they all described places of incredibly intense suffering.

One of those realms that stuck out to Neal above all the others was the domain of the "hungry ghosts." There were two variations in the description, both equally graphic to bring the point home. Imagine a caldron full of a mouthwatering, delicious soup. Surrounding the caldron are starving beings relishing the savory meal that awaited them. But try as they wished, they could not eat the soup. One story tells of a spoon that had a big hole in it, so by the time the utensil reached their mouths, all the contents had leaked out. Or the other version went that the spoon was very large, but their pitiful mouths all had an opening no bigger than a pinhole. Neal recognized there were plenty of hungry ghosts at his job, at the country club, and most certainly even at his church—people with insatiable appetites for money and the power it brought. Was he a hungry ghost? He thought a lot about it.

It was a provocative idea, he thought, this possibility of free will and how we could willingly put ourselves in such states of misery—and just as willingly remove ourselves from those circumstances. But he looked around at the people in his life, his colleagues, his friends, and even his family. And he looked in the mirror at himself. Of course, there were certain elements that were not in our control, things that were not options—like who we had as parents and caregivers as children, whether we had physical or mental illnesses we inherited for which no lifestyle changes would impact, a devastating and unavoidable accident, our exposure to wars, plagues, or famines that we could not outrun, and so on. But there was plenty in our control, where we could make real choices. And we could change our whole attitude about it. The glass was either half-full or half-empty.

He wondered why it was all so hard. Why are the vast majority of us so unhappy and so unwilling to acknowledge or even be aware that we are the architects of our misery and, conversely, of our contentment? Why are we so afraid to abandon the habitual behaviors and thoughts that we know are destructive to ourselves and those around us? Most trudge on through life without pondering these heavy questions, Neal surmised, doing what society expects of them, enslaved by the shared illusion of what success looks like, which often falls short of delivering true happiness or fulfillment. It was one thing to have these contemplations, but it was another thing to do something about it. In this regard, Neal admitted that he was no different from the others. It was like going to church on Sunday, praying, singing, and having an uplifting spiritual experience, only to go back to the life of an unrepentant repeat sinner the rest of the week.

If he was completely honest with himself, Neal would understand why his needle on the meter of happiness only went a few ticks up to the fair classification. He had most certainly far exceeded the trappings most associated with success. Colleagues and subordinates held him in high regard and respect. He had a decent marriage and was proud of the two now-adult offspring it had produced. He never had to think twice about spending on reasonable material indulgences. He had all the creature comforts, the hippest cars, and all the latest gadgets. Maybe his obituary-to-be in the town newspaper would be a fairly boring read, but he had achieved admirable standing, power, and influence in his microcosm.

So, why was he so unsatisfied? Why were the moments of bliss in his life so short and fleeting? Why was liberation something he only felt on the golf course or after the second tumbler of single-barrel whiskey?

The scariest thought for Neal and the best reason for keeping it sealed under lock and key in his soul was the question of who he would be if everything was stripped away. What if a fire came and burned everything around him, and all that was left of his world was himself? Would he curse his fate? Or would he be grateful for surviving and having the chance to begin anew and create something remarkable out of the ashes?

There was little bandwidth in his soul for choice. His whole identity was so entwined with being who he was, being high in the pecking order at the corporation, being the man who all bowed to as he walked down office corridors. In his mind, giving all that up was equivalent to shriveling up and dying. So, as preposterous as it all sounded on face value, his choice of staying put was encoded with a weird instinctual compulsion linked to survival. It didn't help that he saw too many piles of dust, all that was left of some older colleagues and mentors who had been forced to leave because of failing performance. When the time came that he would leave the company, Neal hoped it would be on his own terms.

It was easy to dismiss and defer such troubling thoughts when everything was flowing well and there was more than sufficient recovery time between any fires that needed to be put out. But the crisis-management aspect at work was beginning to make him question whether it was all still worth it. For the time being, he was staying put. The company had been good to him, and he was invaluable to them at this time of need.

Neal was asked by his boss, the CEO, to convene a group within the next week to chart a rapid-response mechanism in the wake of what he termed "a tsunami warning." Because of the internet and the burgeoning rise of a powerful new communications tool called social media, the company needed to respond at lightning speed to attacks on the integrity and quality of its products and the overall trust and goodwill that consumers associated with its name. The company regarded the nascent attacks in the courts and in the media on its products containing talc as a cancer that could metastasize quickly if underestimated or sloppily mishandled.

Neal reached out to the internal public relations chief, who asked if he could bring to the meeting the outside consultant the company had used successfully in past crisis-management cases. Lawyers would also be called upon to brief the group on the status of litigation and relevant strategies. Taking no chances, Neal insisted that a psychologist with expertise on the behavioral patterns of consumers be present. This was not a dress rehearsal or a drill. It was in their faces. It was exactly what he had been expecting and had long feared.

Chapter 11

The absolute worst thing Jane could do in the aftermath of her surgery was to make matters worse for herself. What she couldn't have imagined was that her mind required almost as much healing as her body. It was encouraging with the passing of each day that there was at least one area where she could notice some improvement. Even in the smallest increments, it was still progress. Her state of mind, however, was more of a roller coaster.

Most noticeably, the long zipper of stitches and staples along the side of her torso that produced a tearing pain every time she moved was thankfully becoming more of an itchy, uncomfortable annoyance. Her appointment in a few days to have them removed made her flash back to that indescribable feeling of liberation when the orthodontist removed her braces at age thirteen. No longer was she the awkward and shy girl who hated her metallic smile. This was another passage of sorts, not one overflowing with excitement but one marking the begrudging acceptance of a shrinking existence. Both shared a similar energetic footprint, a heightened sense of discovery. One marked the end of childhood and the beginning of flowering adulthood, while her present reality meant entering a darker portal of uncertainty.

She thought a lot about that thirteen-year-old who never once held the suffering and infirmity of old age and death in her mind stream. In many profound and funny ways, she could trick herself into thinking she was unaltered from her earlier gestalt; her spirit and her outlook on life were remarkably little changed since those teenage years. They both smiled and laughed the same way and at pretty much the same things. They both envisioned a world that was much kinder and fairer and strove to believe in the best sides of humanity despite the enormous scope of misfortune around them.

In her darker moods now, any traces of constructive thinking and positivity floated away in the ethers. Her body had been cracked open, and the same could be said for the joy and contentment that had been her armor in the face of life's daily challenges. Without much warning or provocation, she might suddenly weep out loud. A minor annoyance she would have given little thought to before could suddenly trigger outbursts of explosive magnitude. Even with the explanation from the doctor that such dark mood swings were normal and to be expected during the recovery time, it was absolutely demoralizing to herself and her family. Gone in those moments was the sunny person who was almost always upbeat. It was even more disturbing how her face seemed almost unrecognizable in that state, all of its forty-two muscles appearing hardened and strained with distress. But just as remarkably, those moments would pass almost as quickly as they came. And there was comfort at the return of the loving person they knew. But her husband and children's relief were also tinged with an unspoken sadness and fear, the tenuousness and inevitability of watching a flickering candlelight in the cold wind.

In the loneliness of her condition that seemed impossible to share with others in words, Jane thought about her children when they were small and had no concept of time. How impatient they would become when told to wait for five minutes or during car trips longer than their attention spans. Now, she was the impatient child. "When are we going to get there?" was replaced by "When am I going to get my life back?"

The depression came from the realization that it was all but certain that her life was not coming back, at least not in a very recognizable and acceptable form. All fantasies that she would again hover over a pupil's shoulder with helpful guidance or take a carefree holiday with her husband were gone. Would her grandchildren recoil when seeing her so gaunt and brittle? Would she be able to once again have the strength to do the simplest tasks that brought her joy, like digging in the garden to plant flowers in the spring? The doctor had told her before the surgery that she would regain strength up to a certain degree. But for the moment, she was utterly exhausted, stuck in that back seat. "When are we going to get there?"

On the way to her follow-up appointment with the doctor, Jane asked Phil to drive a little more slowly while navigating a particularly curvy road. She couldn't eat anything that morning at breakfast, and the closer they got to the appointment, the more nauseated she felt. Her mind was absorbed in dread—dread about the pathology report, dread about the treatment plan, dread of the cascading overwhelm of it all and what unpleasant surprises might be in store for her. With what she had been through already, PTSD with all of its gut-wrenching and nerve-wracking side effects was well justified.

The removal of the staples and stitches brought understandable relief. Perhaps it was all psychosomatic, but she felt almost immediately how much easier it was to breathe. As she got up from the examination table, she felt somewhat lighter in spirit and more relaxed in the exertion it took. Now, only the long scarlet scar would be in the mirror as a reminder, lest she could ever forget what had been inflicted upon her. But it was one step, one reassuring little sign that her body still had the mechanism to heal itself, for the tissues to knit themselves back together as whole.

The doctor punched a few strokes on his keyboard to bring up the pathology report on his computer screen. Jane and Phil looked at each other in the silent space as they waited for him to start speaking. The glance was one of mutual agreement, an expectation that nothing the doctor told them would substantially change the situation. Never in their wildest fantasies would he tell them any bright and encouraging news. Similarly, they were not expecting anything worse than what they had already been told.

"The report did confirm that the tumor was a mesothelioma," the doctor said with a clinically neutral and factual tone, like he was reading the weather report. "With the removal of the lung and the tumor inside your chest wall, I think we got it all. The pathologist did not find any tumors in your lymph nodes, which means it is highly unlikely that the tumor has metastasized outside of your chest." He told her that chemotherapy was not recommended in her case since he had done a thorough scrape of the insides of her chest wall, and more importantly due to the clean findings from the pathologist. Before parting, he assured her that it all added up to a much better prognosis and some hope for a longer life.

In any other circumstance, Jane might have walked out of that office feeling a little more cause for optimism, parking her depressive malaise off to the side, at least for the time being. But she was not buying it. His words were not the words of an all-knowing God. She thought perhaps he wanted to leave her with some positive thoughts to slow the flood of stress hormones in her body. Maybe it was also self-serving to lessen his own flood from one of the more uncomfortable parts of his job. At least it wasn't as bad as a priest giving comfort to a death row prisoner before the execution. The only thing she could truly trust was how her body was feeling, not what anyone with an advanced degree told her about what and how she should feel. Everybody was different and often responded differently to the same medicines or the same dosages. And with all their knowledge, no one could give her the answer to the big question: why her? So, if the doctor told her then and there that she had six weeks or six years to live, she would trust neither.

She was quiet the whole ride home, her eyes staring off toward the ceiling of the car, lost in thoughts. It was one big "do not disturb" sign that called for everyone around her to back off and give her slack. Patience and forbearing ruled because everyone knew that it could take several more weeks and perhaps months for her to regain her equilibrium.

About ten days after the appointment, Jane and Phil were watching television in the late evening. Switching off the cable news, Phil channel surfed until they found a program to their mutual taste. It was, of all things, a black-and-white rerun of *Mr. Ed*, a popular show from Jane's childhood about a very opinionated and witty talking horse. It was the first time in a long while that Phil heard Jane laugh. The jokes were still funny more than a half century later.

During a commercial break, Jane was about to get up when Phil motioned for her to stay. He had heard the announcer say, "Have you or a loved one been diagnosed with mesothelioma? You may be entitled to substantial compensation." Phil wrote down the name and phone number listed at the end of the spot. After the program ended, Phil asked her what she thought about the ad. "What do you think? Is it worth a call?"

As often was the case in the evening, Jane wasn't very receptive to anything that would make her feel even more spent and exhausted. "I'm tired. I don't really want to think about it." The next morning at breakfast, she said, "If you want to call that company, go ahead. It may be a scam or a complete waste of time, but check it out if you feel like it."

Chapter 12

Within a few seconds, Phil wondered if he was making a mistake contacting this legal service specializing in mesothelioma cases. He had remembered some twenty-five years before in an unthinking and unguarded moment giving his name and phone number to a seemingly nice and sincere young man on the street. Phil didn't know what Scientology was, but it sounded like something he'd maybe want to check out. The incessant phone calls that ensued, inviting him to various talks and programs, would not cease no matter how many times he told them that he was not interested. Finally, after two years, the phone calls stopped promptly after he threatened taking legal action.

Remarkably and to his pleasant surprise, Phil began to feel more comfortable within a minute or two into the call. Although the person at the law office was clearly working off a script on a computer screen, she entrained her words with what he felt was sincere empathy and sensitivity. No doubt this legal assistant had gone through detailed training on how to be credible, trustworthy, professional, and caring to someone who had been a complete stranger only minutes before. And Phil, likewise, was suddenly divulging deeply personal and confidential information to someone he didn't know from Adam. It made him understand why undertakers usually wore a flower on their black lapels to somehow soften the grim but necessary solemnity of their task. This woman put Phil at ease almost immediately, as though she could read his personality type within seconds, second-guess his concerns, and inspire his confidence.

The questions were at first fairly basic, getting names and contact information as he could hear the legal assistant tapping away on the keyboard. "Are you the patient or is it someone else, and what is your relationship to that person?" "Is this person living or deceased?" "When was she diagnosed, and what was the name of her doctor?" Apologetically, the woman said that she needed a few more details in order to refer him to the best-qualified attorney. She then proceeded to ask many of the same questions they had heard before in the various doctors' offices. Of course, the biggest questions were all about Jane's possible exposures to asbestos, either at work or at home. There was also a brief medical history. When asked about surgeries, Phil mentioned the previous bout with ovarian cancer. He didn't have that information in front of him when asked about dates and doctors. The legal assistant told him not to worry about it.

As the call was winding down, she told Phil that the information he provided met the criteria to move to the next level. She asked him if he would be comfortable getting a call from the lawyer in their area to set up a face-to-face meeting. She added, before Phil even had the time to think about asking, that the consultation with the attorney would be free of charge. Nor was there any obligation to engage the lawyer to represent them.

Phil thought for a few seconds before answering, wondering most of all if he needed to run this by Jane or if he should decide on her behalf. In essence, it wouldn't hurt if he took the next meeting without her, if she didn't feel up to it for any reason. So, it was a no-brainer.

Within twenty-four hours, the phone rang, and Jane answered. The woman on the other end asked to speak with Phil and introduced herself as Emily, an attorney with a law firm not too far from their home. Her husband was at work and would not be home until after six o'clock, Jane told her. From the weakened quality in Jane's voice, Emily knew whom she was talking to. "I would love to meet with you and your husband and see what we can do to help you," she said. Without hesitation, Jane gave her Phil's number at work and asked her to call him to set it up, since she couldn't vouch for his schedule.

A few days later, at the appointed time of nine o'clock on a Monday morning, Emily rang their doorbell. Before sitting down in their living room, she handed each of them her business card. Her last name, to Jane's recognition, had a distinctly Armenian sound to it. The San Fernando Valley had a decent-sized community of people of Armenian heritage, and many of her past students had similar-sounding surnames. So, Jane broke the ice with Emily, talking about her students and parents she had met during the years and all the wonderful food and memorable stories they had shared with her, especially of the plight of their people in Turkey that brought them to America.

"Hearing all those stories from my grandparents is one of the big reasons why I'm sitting with you here today," Emily offered as a means of personal introduction. "I am grateful to live in a country built on laws that work to protect fundamental human rights, unlike what my grandparents faced when they were children. That is one big reason why I became a lawyer." Jane nodded and sat back with a contented smile.

In the time she had with them that morning, Emily told Jane and Phil that she wanted to give them a brief overview of the legal process relating to mesothelioma and then begin to take inventory of the potential determining factors in her case. She explained how the cases of the disease in women were on a disturbing rise, and ones like Jane's with no blatantly obvious smoking gun from direct occupational or environmental exposures was an emerging trend.

Emily opened her laptop to what appeared to be a form and began typing on the keyboard to fill it out. She began by asking about the medical history and occupations of all of Jane's close relatives, whether cancer was prevalent, and specifically if anyone had mesothelioma. In rapid-fire, she then went through a list of risk factors ranging from house renovations and do-it-yourself car repair to hobbies like pottery.

"We've been through this so many times before with the doctors," Phil interrupted. "I can spare you the exercise. The answer to all of these is no."

"I'm sorry to put you through this. But if you want to pursue legal action, I can guarantee that you are going to hear these questions many more times, especially from the attorneys on the other side, and to an annoying degree of detail."

"Have you done any car repairs at home, like changing out the brake pads?"

"No, never."

"Have you frequently used paints and caulking products? Have you done any renovations or remodeling of your home?"

"We did an upgrade on the kitchen and one of the bathrooms, but that was over fifteen years ago."

"OK, we will need to go over that in greater detail."

"You'll need to ask Phil about that, since he oversaw both jobs. I basically stayed out of it."

"That's fine. What about talcum powder? Do you use any products that have talc in it, like baby powder or deodorants?"

"Yes, of course."

"Can you show me these products? Can you take me to your bathroom and show them to me?"

They went upstairs to the bathroom connected to the main bedroom. Jane opened a drawer underneath the countertop and the nearby medicine cabinet and took out a container of a feminine hygiene product to control odor and sweat. Emily wrote down the names of the product and double-checked the ingredients list to confirm.

"How long have you been using this product?"

"More or less as far back as I can remember," Jane answered. "Twenty-five or maybe even thirty years, since it hasn't been around much longer than that. Before then, we used to use baby powder, of course, when the kids were infants."

"How often would you say you use it? How many days a week? Every day, three or four times a week, or what?

"Not as much as I used to, since I'm not going to work any longer, but every workday morning back then for sure."

Returning to the living room, Emily minced no words in giving her assessment. "There's a lot of homework we would need to do, but I do believe this is worth pursuing based on what you've shared with me. In fact, my hunch is that you may have a strong case."

"What makes you think that?" Phil asked. The overriding question he was trying to answer for himself was what exactly they were inviting into their already complicated lives. The big elephant in the room was whether putting Jane through a lawsuit was really a wise choice, given the stress it would place on her. Would that be the best use of whatever time and energy she had left? Might it hasten her decline? Would she ever have any benefit of any monetary settlement? What was the point?

"There is good reason to believe that your use of talcum powder may be the cause of your mesothelioma. The companies that assured you that these products were completely safe have to answer for this. From what we already understand, they knew of the dangers of asbestos in their products for decades and chose to withhold that information from you and countless others. I know you'll want to think about this. You can let me know when you've come to a decision."

Emily started gathering up her papers to put them into her briefcase. She paused for a second to consider whether to say one last thing before leaving.

"There's one other thing I forgot to ask you. When you had the ovarian cancer, did the doctors ever give you any explanation of what might have caused it?"

"No, they told me it was idiopathic. I assume you know what that term means."

"Then there's something more for you to consider," Jane suggested very carefully. "Your doctors probably didn't know it at the time. The asbestos in talc has also been linked to ovarian cancer."

Jane could hardly speak to thank Emily for her time and to say goodbye. Phil walked her to the front door and told her that they would sleep on this overnight and get back to her tomorrow with an answer. As he closed the door, he turned and looked at Jane. He had never seen her look that stunned.

Chapter 13

Since joining her firm two years before, Emily had taken on more than two dozen mesothelioma cases, so she had enough of a sampling to have a keen sense of the psychology of her clients. Every case was different up to a certain point, after which there were fairly predictable patterns of behavior. Clients facing this disease were extraordinarily vulnerable. It was not a simple decision to invite litigation and all the scrutiny into one's life under the best of circumstances. There was the sad, largely unspoken, and undeniable reality of the trickling sand in the hourglass. As crass as it sounded, Emily would have to size up if her new or prospective client would even live long enough to make it to trial. For example, if the court was dealing with a living plaintiff, they would more than likely fast-track it. If the person was on death's doorstep or already deceased, there would be no urgency, and the case on behalf of the estate could drag on for years.

Would someone like Jane have the intestinal fortitude, the strength of will, the conviction and clear motivation to endure a grueling process that would consume many months to reach an outcome? Emily would try to put herself in that situation, whether she would choose to spend the remaining months talking to people like her, dissecting all the minutiae she'd rather forget. Would she willingly want to face the kind of torturous treatment she knew the other side would throw at her?

So, when Emily came into the house of a prospective client, she had a lot of sizing up to do. There was an abundance of information to be gleaned from a host of unspoken clues. Body language could be as good as if not better than a lie detector. Without being obvious, she would study any hint of tension in the face, the positioning and movement of the hands, and how posture could change from one moment to the next, revealing either receptivity or defensiveness. It would guide her on when to be more assertive or more patient, when to push hard or back off.

She also knew that once she entered the door of her client's home, it was all about the client. Authentic compassion was not something she could fake. Her own needs and any stupid, self-indulgent small talk or ego-driven banter were all verboten. And no one really cared if she had her period or a headache that morning or woke up on the wrong side of the bed.

The multimillion-dollar question was always whether the client would be 100 percent in. The way Emily's firm got paid was totally on spec. A tremendous amount of time and resources were invested to prepare and execute a case. So, for that reason, Emily always wanted to conduct her first meeting with as little sales pressure as possible. Any vibe that she was only invested in the final outcome of closing the deal was toxic. If anything, she wanted the prospective client to feel the opposite—how she was only there to help, and above all, she really didn't need the job or the money. Without the pressure of the hard sell, Jane could take her time and come to her own decision. Then, the chances of her backing out midstream would be greatly reduced.

Had she been asked to make a commitment then and there or even later that same day, Jane would have most certainly turned Emily down. It was as if Emily had come into her house and detonated a bomb, reminding her of things she'd rather forget and bursting open old wounds. The ovarian cancer information had been especially incendiary. She had it, she got over it, and the file had been closed. End of story. The theory that somehow her new bout with cancer and the old one claimed a mutual source was overwhelming. How could it be that she had been so forgiving and fatalistic about a disease of unknown origin? *That's just the way it goes, the luck of the draw*, she had rationalized.

Jane did not recognize herself in the emotions she was feeling. It was one thing to be sick, exhausted, and trying to make peace with her mortality. Suddenly, layered onto her already full plate was indignation, rage, and demoralization. There were murderers at large, plundering and stealing all that she cherished.

Phil took the rest of that day off work, on ready standby for what might come. In some respects, he considered it the most challenging and difficult decision they had ever faced, more than consenting to major surgeries. And in his own shell-shocked condition, he didn't even know how he himself would answer the question. Never for a moment would he want to put any pressure on her to fight or not fight. He could never imagine living with the guilt if she looked at him on her deathbed and said, "Why did you make me do this!" Just like Emily had done, Phil needed to give her all the time and space to make up her mind. He knew in either scenario he would have to be a loyal foot soldier, as if this might be the very last big thing she might ever ask him to do in their lifetime together.

Jane engaged herself for the rest of the day in what could only be considered mindless busywork. It was better than taking a sedative. Household chores that were normally her least favorite things to do were suddenly high priority. Emptying the dishwasher. Vacuuming. Folding laundry. Cleaning the oven. Sorting the sock drawer. She didn't bring up the topic all day. Powering through all her tasks on one lung would hopefully exhaust her enough so she wouldn't have to lie awake thinking about it at night as well, she hoped.

When she woke up in bed the next morning, she felt like her comforter weighed a thousand pounds. It had not been a restful sleep, although she was thankful that the night had passed quickly and undisturbed.

At breakfast, she told Phil that she wanted to call Emily that morning. She didn't want to go through another day carrying the weight of this on her shoulders, she told him. "It all boils down to, what's the right thing to do," she explained. "What's the right thing for me? What's the right thing to do for you, for our children and grandchildren? What's the right thing for all the others who are going through the same thing? What's the right thing to do toward the perpetrators? And what do I want all of you to think about me long after I'm gone? What did I stand for? What did I do in this horrible moment? What will give me ultimate peace?"

An hour later, Jane called Emily. "When can we meet? I'm ready to move forward."

Chapter 14

Emily placed her laptop computer on the dining room table in front of her to ready herself to type in Jane's responses to more detailed questionnaires specific to her type of case. This information gathering was a crucial first step in the process to prepare the interrogatories, a document comprised of very detailed questions and answers for inclusion in the initial court filing. It was essentially all the nuts and bolts of the case that condensed every single factor in the plaintiff's world that could have bearing on the ultimate outcome. Each item was annotated with names, dates, and other identifiers whenever appropriate, so it could all be easily fact-checked if in dispute. The information would be also provided to the defense as part of their discovery.

Jane was fully warned that this was one of those parts of the job that was tedious but mandatory. It was like running the first few steps of a marathon. Starting anything new easily created apprehension that could spiral into anxiety and fear, especially with something as arduous as this appeared at face value. It was an open-ended commitment with no apparent off-ramp.

Emily did everything she could to assure Jane that trepidation was a natural and expected response. This was understandably all new to her. A big part of Emily's job was to be a human shield against some of the ruthless, despicable sides of humanity manifest in the legal arena. Although the age difference between them was more than thirty years, Emily became the mother, handholding and protecting Jane in her vulnerable, childlike state.

It didn't take long for Jane to see how every single nook and cranny of her life was going under the microscope. Stuff about her life and her medical history that no one would have interest or cause to know would soon become public record, an open book. It started out with the basic stuff, like filling in her Social Security number, names, ages, and employment histories of immediate family members, both alive and deceased, dating back to her grandparents' generation. Before they would finish two days later, the dissection of all the relevant intimate details of her life would be complete, at least for the moment.

While Emily typed away, Jane was admonishing herself to have patience, take deep breaths, and deal with the process as unpleasant as it was. It reminded her of when she was in college, picking up a few quick dollars doing annual inventory for a department store. The clock on the wall moved in slow motion. It was torturous counting all the merchandise, large and small, for hours on end. She somehow got through it and hoped it would be no different this time around. Now, she was doing inventory on her life. Emily assured her that the more thorough they were, the less fodder there would be for the other side to stir up things once litigation was in full swing. The less she said, "I don't recall" or "I don't remember," the more credible her case would seem to the jury.

Emily needed her own hacks to get through this least-favorite part of her job. She equated it to the painstaking prep work a housepainter needed to do before ever touching a wet brush to a wall. Without it, the mediocre results would speak for themselves. Caffeine and maintaining a good sense of humor on both sides helped. It could be dull and even deadening in its routine but sometimes full of surprises when a big discovery happened that helped to better connect the dots. On the other side of the table, she had to stay tuned in to Jane's energy level, looking for even a hint of fatigue from her client, especially important on this, their first day. Better to err on the side of caution and call it quits a few minutes too early rather than risk overstaying her welcome.

Everyone Emily had represented had their own threshold of how long they could stay in the zone until brain fog happened and quickly degenerated the whole thing into diminishing returns. Some could talk for hours with no signs of tiring, while others seemed to reach their limit after two hours or even less. Sometimes she would come over, and clients would drop it on her that they were in bad shape that day and needed to reschedule.

Before she left the meeting that first day, Emily had enough material to at least get the wheels in motion. She had gone through in exhaustive detail the list of all the health care providers Jane had seen from her childhood, ferreting out who might have treated Jane for any relevant conditions or symptoms, operations and procedures, pathology and lab reports, anything in the way of corroborating documents to support the case. Jane signed all the necessary permissions and releases so Emily could hand the grunt work off of hunting down these records to her paralegal.

What impressed Jane more than anything and caught her a little bit by surprise was how Emily dove into the what artists call the negative space. When we look at the painting of a beautiful vase of flowers, for example, what we sometimes fail to appreciate is the space around the object—overlooking the importance of the shadows, contour, and perspective that elevate it from simple illustration into dynamic art. So, as much as Emily wanted to cull through all Jane's medical records for anything that could prove her case, she had equal priority to preemptively find things that could be used by the opposition to shoot holes. The negative space to look at here was making sure nothing pointed to another cause of her condition, no matter how minute or far-fetched, data that might build the other side's case that there were other culprits over Jane's lifetime that could have potentially triggered her mesothelioma.

It is the same reason why information about Jane's family over the span of her lifetime was also important. "Did your father or mother, aunts and uncles, and cousins have jobs or hobbies that could have brought asbestos into your home?" Emily asked her to give this careful thought, telling her that they had time and could continue to add new information if she recalled anything else in the coming days. She rattled off the list of the usual suspects they had discussed before, now to have it on the record and official: ceramics, car repair, home construction and renovation, frequent exposure to paints and caulking, and so on. It was a big fat no to it all. Jane could not think of a single situation.

Emily explained why this was important. After all, mesothelioma wasn't an acute onset disease caused by a brief exposure to a dangerous environmental toxin. In almost all cases, it could take thirty, forty, or even fifty years of regular exposure to asbestos to cause the disease, excluding those in professions working with asbestos in very high concentrations. Therefore, this vast pool of information needed to be carefully combed through.

When they got together the next morning, the focus of the new day was on the history of Jane's use of products with talcum powder. Emily was even more convinced after the process of elimination from yesterday's questioning that talcum powder was the probable (and only) cause. It was her job to fully detail and document Jane's history of use of these products.

Like the day before, most of these questions were methodical and followed a predictable pattern. "What product did you use? Where did you apply it? How much did you apply? How often?" It was embarrassing for Jane to talk about anything related to her bodily functions.

"I tend to perspire a lot," she told Emily, uncomfortably shifting in her seat, wondering if she had ever divulged this to another human. It had been applied to prevent sweating and to absorb the moisture on her neck, under her arms, under her breasts, and between her legs.

"Are they going to grill me in the courtroom about this? This is super creepy to me."

"It's something that you will unfortunately have to get used to," Emily explained. "Maybe before then, we will have gone through this enough that you will become desensitized. We need to get this right. This type of testimony is of utmost importance, and trust me, at trial, the defense will look for contradictions, inconsistencies, or any other weaknesses in even the smallest details."

Jane pointed out that she couldn't remember a time when she didn't use talcum powder. "I remember seeing my mother put it on my baby sister as a newborn, so I have to assume she did the same to me." She described how she had used the baby powder throughout her childhood, teenage years, and early adulthood, switching to the adult versions once they were available in the marketplace. "It was just a normal thing to do. You woke up, brushed your teeth, washed your face, combed your hair, and put the powder in your hand and rubbed it in on all those places where it was needed. It was so automatic. It was never something any of us gave any thought to. And the idea that it could harm us in any way was the furthest thing from our minds."

"Did you ever see any warnings about the health hazards of talc, on labels or even in a newspaper or magazine?"

"No. Never."

Emily went on to ask about cosmetics, since makeup products contain talc from many of the same sources. "How often did you use facial bases?" She also asked about eye makeups, which commonly use talc to absorb moisture, smooth the consistency, and prevent caking. "Not daily, if that's what you mean. Maybe a little eye shadow, but I've never been one to use a lot of makeup," Jane answered. "Maybe I might use a little more if we were going out to a party or to a fine restaurant but rarely more than once a week," she added. Before leaving the topic, Emily asked how she applied the products to ascertain the degree to which the particles might end up in the air and be inhaled.

In that same regard, some of her questioning toward the end was puzzling to Jane. "Why do you want to know so much about the cleaning of my bathroom?"

Emily explained that her exposure from the talcum powder was not limited to the initial application. "The dust persists on your counter, your floors, and your furniture," she explained. "It's almost like secondhand smoke from a cigarette—maybe not as bad as the primary exposure but a health risk all the same. Every time you wipe the counter or run the vacuum cleaner over the floor, those talc particles become airborne again and have another chance to get into your body. There has been some recent research on this that really brings home how sinister this effect can be."

As they wrapped up the session, Jane looked like she had to get something off her chest. "Do you mean to tell me that all those years, they knew all along they were selling me deadly poison?"

"Sadly, that's true. My guess is that they never thought they'd get caught. It doesn't help that doctors rarely ask their patients if they ever used talcum powder or had other exposures to asbestos either themselves or via a family member. Remember how your doctor shrugged his shoulders and called your ovarian cancer idiopathic, just as they do in around 70 percent of the cases. Women are especially victimized in this regard, since they are much bigger consumers of talcum powder compared to men, although men who use talc are just as vulnerable. But I'm willing to bet that the vast majority of these women, just like you, with no other asbestos risk factors, used significant amounts of talcum powder on their bodies, faces, or both."

Chapter 15

After a few more phone conversations, Emily had what she needed from Jane to begin preparing a good portion of the necessary legal documents to file with the court. There was a formula to all of this that left very little to chance, following a boilerplate based on the fundamentals of jurisprudence and adjusted to any recent court rulings that might have altered precedent. A good deal of what Emily needed to do was fill in the blanks that differentiated Jane's case from all the others.

As she went through her mental checklist, Emily could not be more pleased. Her expectations of Jane from their meetings were gold. Jane was intelligent, credible, succinct, unwavering, and consistent in her answers. And she was a likeable person the jury would view sympathetically. If there was any anger felt, it was coming from a resigned but clear place of righteous indignation. It was an intensity that most juries could easily sympathize with and consider appropriate and justified.

Emily also put Jane to the test in terms of her stamina to endure the stress of questioning both from a mental and physical standpoint. She was fully cognizant that Jane's condition could worsen on a dime, but the snapshot she had was of someone who was fully sound and capable. For those reasons and more, time was of the essence, especially for the courts of California that customarily fast-tracked cases with living plaintiffs.

Jane, for her part, erased any doubts she might have had regarding the decision to move forward. She felt Emily was sincere and sensitive and had her heart in the right place and for the right reasons. Yes, there were considerable dollars at stake and to be made from a successful outcome in this case. That was the way of the world. But as she felt before, and now only stronger, there was a social justice statement to be made that was more valuable to Jane than the money she herself would probably have precious little opportunity to enjoy. She felt emboldened. Talking with Phil afterward, she mused that maybe having this purpose might strengthen her and keep her healthier and more vital. There were plenty of stories of people who outlived doctors' prognoses because their sense of mission overrode the disease, at least in the short term.

If it wasn't already clear to Jane, it would soon be established that her case rose in magnitude for the simple reason that she had two separate cancers in all probability linked to the same cause—and traced to the same source of corporate negligence and malfeasance. As Emily would later explain to her, it wasn't that these cases were unheard of, but they were quite rare and therefore more newsworthy. What possibly happened to Jane was tantamount to getting struck by lightning not once but twice. Again, it happened but was rare and dumbfounding. "Just think, your wife may become a poster child," Jane quipped to her husband.

The paralegal had urgent marching orders to reach out to Jane's doctors and the hospitals where her surgery and treatments had been done. All the records and lab reports were crucial to have on hand for the court filing and subsequent review by the defense attorneys' experts. The highest priority of all was to track down any preserved tissue samples from Jane's surgeries from the hospitals. These needed to be sent for analysis by a pathologist with expertise in talc and asbestos cases. This could take time and potentially be mired in legal delays requiring court orders if the hospital pathology department declined to cooperate. Many of them had cancer research projects of their own and had competing interests to preserve those tissues for their own studies.

Ten days later, the pathologist at a major university hospital in New York City received the first of two parcels containing Jane's tissue samples. The hospital in California where Jane had her hysterectomy had packed the shipment in a cold-pack Styrofoam container to ensure that it would arrive undamaged. Although the surgery had been done almost eight years earlier, the hospital had followed the national protocol of preserving the specimens for at least a decade if not longer.

The bulk of the work in the laboratory was not handed off to a skilled technician but done by a pathologist named Paul. Everything that took place there would be subject to an intense level of scrutiny in a courtroom. The lawyer for the defense would look to dissect the smallest of details to uncover any procedural missteps to sow doubt in the validity of the findings.

By this point, Paul knew every trick in the trade. He was the go-to pathologist when it came to mesothelioma cases. He had already been on the witness stand three hundred times and counting. So, the simple step of opening the box and removing the contents was something he did with clockwork precision. There were accession numbers assigned to each tissue sample that were not only time-stamped and recorded in a book but photographed as well. There were original pathology reports and often histological microscope slides corresponding to each sample to also keep in order.

Contrary to what one might think, specimens from Jane's tumors were not of primary interest to Paul. The damage he was looking for was more telling in the surrounding tissues. The malignant tumor caused as a response to the asbestos fibers was a relatively new growth growing around it. Studying a lymph node, for example, would usually yield a higher fiber particle count and therefore tell a more conclusive story.

Inside the shipment were twenty paraffin blocks of embedded tissue from Jane's reproductive system. Measuring an inch on all sides, the first thing Paul needed to do was divide each of the blocks in half, keeping one piece for his analysis and the other half preserved for possible study by an expert hired by the defense. Where he made the cut had to be carefully executed. The defense might weakly argue they didn't get an adequate amount. Neither was there any way of telling whether the two halves would have equal or similar properties, or whether one side might skew a significantly higher asbestos fiber count than the other. Paul did not lose any sleep over the minimal chances of that happening.

The next stage was to bring the preserved tissue sample back to life or as close to something mimicking the condition of a freshly removed specimen. A lab technician dissolved the paraffin when the tissue was embedded with the solvent xylene. Then it was immersed in alcohol to remove the xylene. Water was then added as the final step to restore the tissue to a somewhat natural state, minus the cell membranes and fatty lipid portions of the cells that also dissolved in the process. The tissue was then blotted dry and weighed.

From there, the process was to digest any and all of the biologic materials in the tissues, leaving only inorganic compounds. To achieve this, the specimen was minced up into small pieces and soaked in a caustic solution. What remained was a liquid that was run in a centrifuge that spun at high speeds to separate the fluids from inorganic minerals or metal materials. The liquid now consisted of water, and the caustic solution was poured out. The pellet at the bottom of the tube was washed five times in distilled water and centrifuged to ensure all biologic material and caustic solution was gone. After the final wash, it was resuspended in a known small amount of distilled water and then oscillated in a sonicator so that the ten microliter drops put onto electron microscopic grids were uniform and representative of the whole sample.

For the shipment of lung and chest cavity tissues Paul received the following week, the prep work right up to the mincing stage was unnecessary. The tissues looked much the same from the day they had been cut from Jane's body, preserved in formalin and encased in sealed containers. Paul removed representative portions from the lung and dissected out the lymph nodes central for his analysis.

Each grid Paul made was coded much like a road map that uses a longitudinal letter and a latitudinal number running on the margins of the page, consisting of ten on each side, with one hundred squares in total. In this case, the grid provided the reference points to easily locate, identify, quantify, and catalogue the findings in his report. The grids were put into a grid holder for loading into the electron microscope.

Under the powerful microscope, the grid would go through three successive processes to progressively narrow down the content. The first was to identify the structure, notably either fibrous or amorphous. Then that structure was analyzed by EDS (energy dispersive spectrography), an electron microscopic accessory that identified the elements and the relative amount of each element. Because many of the fibers looked alike, a third process called SAED (selected area electron diffraction) made it possible with greater precision to identify the type of fiber or particle, based on its crystalline structure, differentiating between those commonly found in cosmetic products versus ones found in industrial exposures. These criteria all together were the most effective means of identifying which type of asbestos was seen and identified the specific amorphous particles. The conclusions made by Paul made it possible to correlate what was found in Jane's tissue with what was found in the containers of the talcum powder and cosmetics Jane used.

The final step involved some heavy math as Paul counted the structures seen in each square on the grid, up to eight hundred grid openings for each tissue tested. The results were entered into a formula to determine how many of those fibers or particles would be seen in the entire preparation. By the end of the process, it was possible to see if those particles truly matched the exposure history.

Sometimes, especially if the patient hadn't used talc products for many years but developed mesothelioma from this prior damage, Paul might not find the smoking gun. They could have had sufficient exposure to develop mesothelioma for thirty years, but if they had stopped using it a decade prior to the tissue removal, those components of asbestos fibers and talc could have been digested and/or moved. The half-life of chrysotile asbestos and talc (the asbestos seen in some talc) was only one to three years. However, this would not be the case with the more common asbestos types, tremolite and anthophyllite, which would be clearly seen if present. If Paul's findings got into some of these gray areas, the testimony from other experts would have great importance, such as an industrial hygienist who could cite scientific models on all the risk factors of extensive daily use.

Paul wrote up his findings and sent them off to Emily to review with Jane. He had a good feeling he'd be meeting them both in person some months later in a courtroom.

When she got the report, Emily called her client with the news. Paul's report had concluded that tremolite and anthophyllite asbestos consistent with talc exposure was found in the examination of both the ovarian and the lung area tissues.

"We have a case," Emily advised her. "Do you want me to move forward?"

"Yes. I want this. They need to answer for this."

Chapter 16

The head of the legal team at the company asked to meet with Neal. At this point, there were more than one hundred lawsuits they were handling, all related in some way to their products containing talc. There was a system in place to handle it, the creation of which Neal had helmed. They had hired a network of top litigators with sharp teeth, the best money could buy. Similarly, they had locked up a number of leading scientists and doctors, flying them into various jurisdictions to appear in court, wielding a powerful flyswatter.

From Neal's point of view, the strategy of containment was working according to plan. Yes, these were fires that needed to be put out. But they were only blazes that could be encircled and doused quickly. He had seen situations like this come and go with a "this too shall pass" attitude. It also helped that it hadn't reached any critical mass of societal concern. The general public was not talking about it.

What also helped was that the media did not seem all that interested. There were no bombshell exposés and nothing on the internet resembling a viral outbreak. Neal knew from being in the trenches that news stories could float under the radar for indefinite periods. But then suddenly, without much warning, a piece could appear in a respected medical journal that could upset the apple cart. Health and medical journalists were often loath to report on uncorroborated stories without the protective cover of such peer-reviewed findings.

But for the time being, all was quiet. The whole story seemed tainted and cheapened by the plethora of direct-response television ads for mesothelioma law firms, bedfellows with "I've fallen, and I can't get up" alarm systems and super-duper power washers to remove stubborn household grime. There was also the dilution factor; the company was not the only one making popular products with talc. Some of their biggest competitors were also lawyering up.

If the complaint made it to court, there were so many variables and other considerations that made the claims against the company very challenging to prove. When looking at a disease progression many decades in the making, there were so many different factors to look at that could weaken the company's culpability in a decisive way. So far, the lawyers for the company were earning their keep. The damage to the brand had been minimal at worst. The corporate behemoth regarded it as a bothersome mosquito capable of scoring a bite and sucking a few drops of blood before being promptly smashed to a pulp.

On an interpersonal level, Neal was not losing any sleep over all of this. His carefully orchestrated plan was testing well. The senior-most upper management and board of directors were not breathing down his neck about it. Nor did he feel any pangs of personal responsibility for what was taking place. He would be the last to admit that it was a kind of Nuremberg defense. He was truly only following orders. He did not consider himself a coldhearted bastard who didn't feel sympathy for human suffering, but …

What made it any different from if he was in a military command center in a mountain in Colorado, pressing a button to unleash a deadly missile or drone on the other side of the world that would kill scores of faceless people—and then going home to his wife and kids for dinner like nothing had happened? Neal had been hermetically sealed from the company's accusers, not personally involved to any degree—and he certainly wanted to keep it that way.

When looking at the global broad strokes of what it stood for and the collective benefit of all of its products, the company regarded this situation as both a bagatelle in its bottom line yet also as a point of honor worth defending. However, not to be spoken about above a whisper were some hidden agendas that were less than wholesome for the company's rosy-cheeked, family-friendly image.

If an old acquaintance reunited with Neal after twenty years, the only difference they would notice about him was the result of the natural aging process. Gravity was winning according to the folds in his neck, the sag in his jowl, and the bulge in his midriff. His hair was gray, and his walk was more carefully measured. He had one of those plastic pill sorters to remind him to take his prescriptions for a range of conditions he was so far able to keep in check. He had one pill for prediabetes, another for high blood pressure, a statin for his cholesterol, and a fourth to regulate his thyroid. Despite all of that, he felt robust enough to believe that nothing was going to slow him down.

He still insisted on not using a golf cart, unlike his feebler contemporaries. He got out to the gym barely enough to keep muscle loss at bay and do the cardio work his doctor recommended. Debilitating chronic disease was something that happened to other people, often brought on by their bad lifestyle choices that aggravated their family genetic history, he believed.

His attitude did not exactly make him more sympathetic to these faceless people who had grievances against the company. Shit happens. You can die of an overdose if you drink too much water. So what if you get something after using talcum powder for forty or fifty years? If it was really that dangerous, wouldn't the cases mount into the many millions? What about all the pesticides we're eating and breathing? What about all those thousands of chemical compounds (many surely toxic) that are in the environment and consequently in our bloodstream that didn't exist in our grandparents' generation? Why single out talc as a cause when we've already poisoned and compromised our immune systems beyond belief? Maybe all these talcum powder cases are just the tipping factor of a host of crap already stressing out our bodies. This rationale, whether partially based in hard science or just his own conviction, pacified his conscience and made him feel like the company was being unfairly singled out.

"There's a case in California we may need to pay particular attention to," the lawyer told Neal as he handed him the court brief. "They're claiming that a woman got both ovarian cancer and pleural cancer traced to our talc. It's filed in the superior court in the county of Los Angeles. Somebody is in all certainty going to pick this up. It could blow up."

Chapter 17

Phil answered the doorbell. Waiting on the doorstep was a videographer who introduced himself and asked where he should set up his equipment. Moments later, he brought in his video camera, a tripod, and a lighting kit into the living room. He also hooked up a speaker box and telephone-conferencing panel, the latest technology that would accommodate participants who would not be able to attend that day in person.

Depositions were usually dry and boring affairs, anal for the extreme of detail they craved. The process was more than just a dress rehearsal for the real trial in front of the judge. It was a chance for both sides to fully examine the case through the various witnesses' and experts' accounts, so that there would be no surprises later on. The sworn testimony would give a baseline to know what everyone knew and would help the attorneys on both sides to sharpen their cases.

Coming into Jane's living room that day also had a far more serious purpose. Far too often, plaintiffs might suddenly take a turn for the worse and not be able to testify in the court trial. This was an insurance policy so the jury could see Jane and hear her side of the story if she became incapacitated or deceased. There was also good reason from the plaintiff's side for doing it in Jane's home rather than a more impersonal conference room in the attorney's office suite. Seeing all the personal effects, such as family portraits in the background, would subliminally underscore the fact that this was a real human being, someone with whom the jury could more easily relate and sympathize.

As much as she wasn't looking forward to what she imagined would be a grueling process, Jane was relieved that it was finally underway. No longer was this matter a hypothetical, but she nevertheless hoped it would be over quickly. In her life, she had never been involved in any legal matter more serious than a speeding ticket. Her impressions were mostly colored from friends and colleagues who had shared with her their seemingly never-ending divorce cases. The usual takeaway with most was how there were no winners. After all the aggravation and legal bills, what remained was only a sense that the victorious party would emerge a little less beat up than the other. But it was a parallel she could only take so far. Her friends went on living, sometimes much for the better and with a fresh start after their cases settled. Death and dying was another matter, and all she could count on was the debilitation and pain and the ominous ticking clock.

What girded Jane to go through with it with a bring-it-on attitude was that she did not want the perpetrators to have the last laugh on her. Through the prism of her community charity work, Jane had a solid introduction to corporate mentality and behavior. When she asked for a grant or a sponsorship, it was naïve to believe it would be awarded out of a totally benevolent spirit. There was what she called go-away money, the gift of a small amount to get off the phone, tossing a bone so she wouldn't bother them again for a good while. Any larger grants were usually justified from a more direct and self-interested marketing strategy. Short of that, she might get shuffled off to the corporation's foundation and wait for a turndown form letter.

"They're never going to change what they're doing out of the goodness of their hearts," Jane had opined to Phil after dinner one evening, talking about the upcoming case. "But if it hits them in the pocketbook, maybe they will, and then perhaps everything we're doing here will matter."

Jane greeted all the intruders that day with a sense of calm and assurance. On one end, she was not trying to pull the wool over anyone's eyes. The facts from her experience spoke for themselves and were undeniable. Just as she had all of her life, she optimistically trusted that the truth would prevail. At the same point, nothing was certain in that "life is not always fair" world.

Emily had given her an orientation on what to expect to minimize any surprises or being struck off guard. "Keep your answers short and to the point," she emphasized. "The other side is looking for any daylight for even the slightest inconsistencies or ambiguities that might give a jury pause to doubt your credibility. Again, it is not about being evasive or unforthcoming, but the more embellishment you give, the more you open the doorway to unwelcome scrutiny. Pay particular note that what you say here will be consistent with your testimony on the stand once the trial is underway. They will be looking out for that. You will also have the chance to review the transcript of your deposition and correct any details in case you erred on something or get a clearer memory."

What was more perplexing to Jane was the fact that Neal's company was not the only defendant in her trial. How could it matter that incidental exposure to some paint and caulking products home remodelers had used more than twenty years ago over a cumulative period of several weeks would have any bearing on her case?

"That seems like such a complete waste of everybody's time," Jane complained.

"What you have to keep in mind is our primary defendant is going to want to shift the responsibility to others and maintain they were not the cause of your mesothelioma. By including the other manufacturers, we will make sure these arguments are addressed and resolved."

As soon as the defense attorney arrived in person and the lawyers for the lesser parties dialed in, the proceedings began. Emily began the questioning. The first order of business was to establish that Jane felt well enough to participate and was not on any medication that might impair her abilities. Other formalities included giving her name, address, number of years at that residence, list of family members, date and location of birth, other cities she had lived in, education, name of husband, date of marriage and details about her children and grandchildren, their occupations, and so on.

There were also a number of family photographs that were entered into the record as exhibits, showing Jane at different stages of her life from childhood to the present. All of the pictures, with the exception of the most recent one, projected an image of glowing health and vitality: a happy three-year-old with big rosy cheeks, an engaging and energetic high school student, a beautiful bride in a wedding portrait, and a beaming young mother with her firstborn. The last photo of her playing with one of her grandchildren offered a disturbing contrast, displaying the ravages of disease, a strained smile on a gaunt face.

It was a fitting springboard for Emily's line of inquiry into the history of Jane's diseases, dating back to the diagnoses, through all the surgeries and treatments, to her condition at present. Jane recounted her entire medical history, speaking in graphic detail about what it felt like to be inside her body. To a fly on the wall, it was a saga of unimaginable pain and suffering that one would not wish on one's worst enemy. It was enough to go through one major cancer in a lifetime, but to be hit with two separate attacks was catastrophic. The fact that she was persevering, patient, sincere, and cogent in her answers was in itself a revealing portrait of her resilient spirit and character.

There was a part of her that was both curious and strangely empathetic toward the defense attorneys. "I would not want to have their jobs to try to shoot holes in an already half-dead wreck." She laughed at the thought of it in her mind. Outside of interrupting with various objections to some of Emily's questions, the opposing attorney present and his colleagues on the phone remained mostly silent that day. Their turn would come at the following session tomorrow. They had agreed that they would limit Jane's testimony to no more than two hours, and the time had now elapsed.

Chapter 18

It could be said that fearful anticipation is often the more bitter-tasting medicine than the actual event itself. Jane fully expected the second day of her deposition to be a lot more grueling and contentious, since it would look to dissect the minutiae of her daily life over a few decades that were central to the case. Much of the previous session had been taken up with a more general foundation for her case, so it had been a gentler on-ramp to the process. What had surprised Jane was how something so strange the day before, having a video camera and attorneys in her living room, now seemed like the most normal thing in the world.

As the questioning would be veering into the more specific factors of her asbestos exposure, Jane anticipated that the cordial and collegial tone between the attorneys might start to get testy. There were frequent objections to the way questions were worded that would be arbitrated by the judge at a later time. But overall, Jane was surprised and relieved that it never seemed to get personal in an inflammatory way between the opposing counsels. It could be that some of them knew each other from previous cases. She thought there was a surely a code of ethics and conduct they had learned in law school. Or even more likely, they all understood that appearing more sensitive was a good thing if any of this material might be screened later on for the jury. Above and beyond, they all without exception went out of their way to wear kid gloves when questioning Jane, so as to not be seen as heartless and deplorable.

Emily cracked up later when Jane told her of her surprise that adversaries could be so friendly. "You're not alone. I once had a client who started hyperventilating during her deposition. We, of course, stopped the proceedings and asked her if she was OK. It turned out she got a terrible anxiety attack because she thought we were being too friendly to each other."

There would be no hardball techniques, no badgering, and no personal attacks in her home over the course of these two days. No one was faulting the fact that Jane was deathly ill and that asbestos was indisputably the cause of at least one of her cancers. Their task instead was passing the buck, denying and deflecting any intimation that their products had been the cause of Jane's disease.

Emily started off the session by having Jane talk in painstaking detail about everything that anybody would want to know about her use of talc-based cosmetic products. There were no stones left unturned and no consideration for any sense of privacy. Phil might have been married to her for almost four decades, but he only knew the broad strokes of her intimate hygiene regimen behind the closed bathroom door. But now it would be in the public record that her mother gave her the first bottle when she started having her period at age thirteen. That she applied approximately a teaspoon to her vaginal area every day until very recently, when she found out about the health risks. For good measure, she dusted the inside of her shoes for sweat and odor control and put a light layer under her armpits.

Describing her daily ritual, Jane told all the parties how pleasant the scent from the powder was. Its subtle fragrance was fresh and unintrusive, especially to those around her who might be sensitive to perfumes and colognes. Never once did she have any doubt about the safety of the product, no more than she could imagine getting mouth cancer from her toothpaste. There were a host of products she used in her house for cleaning, laundry, dusting, and polishing that had been in her family's cabinets for generations. Trust was never in doubt, and integrity was never questioned, she emphasized in her testimony.

Emily made a particular point to ask how the family handled their housecleaning chores, specifically relating to the bathroom where Jane applied the talcum. "Did you clean the bathroom and the rest of the home yourself, or did you hire someone else?"

Jane replied that she had only had a service come in once a month for a deep cleaning, and in between, she did a weekly vacuuming. "I'm a stickler on the bathroom and the kitchen," she said. "They have to be immaculate." Emily asked Jane to describe in detail how she cleaned the bathroom, especially about wiping the counters and whether she swept the floor or vacuumed. "Once I got sick and had the surgeries, I no longer had the strength to do it, so we had to have extra help."

To Jane's astonishment, the company's attorney did not choose to cross-examine her. He was a bespectacled, button-down collared, fortyish-year-old man named Miles, who could have been an older and slightly graying Armani model in *Esquire* magazine. Emily assured her after the session as they quickly debriefed that Miles or one of his other colleagues would not remain muted for long. It was all part of a strategy to lay back and save their ammunition for later on at trial. Furthermore, she explained, the defense would do all he could to marginalize Jane's importance, focusing instead on attacking the experts, casting doubt on the veracity of their findings and discrediting the testing techniques.

The final hour of Jane's deposition was dominated by attorneys representing two of the products used in Jane's home during the renovation of her kitchen and bathroom. Here the questioning was more aggressive, as their desired outcome was to throw buckets of cold water on any claims of negligence on their side. It was their hope that on the strength of the deposition alone, a judge might throw out the case against them, leaving the talcum powder as the sole suspect. Their questions demanded detailed answers, many of which were so far in the past and so erased in memory that they were impossible to answer.

What Jane could recall was being present in the home while the repairs were taking place and not away on a vacation. "Were you around and in the presence of the workers when they mixed the powders for the filler to patch the drywall or adhesives to attach tilework?" Jane could not recall any specific recollections but made the general comment that she was curious about what they were doing and looked in on them frequently.

What she could remember was that she cleaned up after the workers after each day. It was an undeniable fact that the residue from the job had a way of infiltrating the rest of the house if left to pile up, migrating from floors to carpets. The dust might also spread to the other rooms through the home's ventilation ducts.

They also asked her how she could be sure that it was their products that had been used. "That's easy." She smiled. "There were opened boxes left over after the jobs were finished, and we kept them in the garage. After complaining to my husband for years about why we needed to keep them, he finally agreed we could throw them out, and so we did, maybe about five years ago."

Jane was relieved when everyone was gone. The last portion was exhausting for her due to its tedium. There would be many more hours of depositions to go, but thankfully, her part was finished. The next time she would be put under oath and have to answer more attorney questions would be in front of a judge and jury.

Chapter 19

Jane received a series of bulky envelopes from Emily over several weeks. Inside were stacks of papers separated into thick files. Jane had requested to see all the transcripts from the depositions in her case. It was a first for Emily. It was a more common practice for the corporate defendant to want to go through all the plaintiff side's depositions. Most of her clients trusted that she would sift carefully through all the materials and call to her attention anything noteworthy. They probably felt they had better things to do with the precious days remaining than to trample in such weeds.

"I hope I'm not a nuisance to you," Jane explained when making the request. "But I think it would make me better prepared to know where they're coming from. I don't pretend that I'll understand everything, but I think it will give me a good feel. I'm curious about how all these people will be dissecting me."

Unlike her deposition, the rest were not videotaped. The jury would have the chance to see some of those witnesses or experts in person in the courtroom, which was obviously not a sure thing given Jane's precarious health. Much of the material, unless cited directly in the courtroom proceedings, would never rise above the level of background information. And in some cases, a number of those deposed would not end up appearing in court if their testimony was not considered crucial to the case.

Having a client who actively wanted to be informed was better than the opposite scenario. Jane had already proven herself a stellar witness—natural, sympathetic, articulate, and highly likeable. If she were too studied, perhaps there would be a chance some of those attractive attributes could be compromised. But the last thing Emily wanted was to be discouraging when a client showed this level of interest.

Reading some of this material in such stark and cold clinical terms ran the risk of being too jarring. On the other hand, Jane reckoned perhaps it was good to get desensitized up front since the content of courtroom testimony would be no less disturbing. And if she could become more of a neutral onlooker, she might appreciate the strategy that went into it all. In this regard, it was a rather cruel game of chess; the only difference, of course, was that it wasn't a friendly pastime. The pieces moving around the board were human beings. And there was a lot of money at stake. Almost everyone had some financial interest in participating, charging hundreds of dollars per hour for their time. Jane was amused by the fact that the defense made such a big deal in the depositions to grill the plaintiff's expert witnesses on how much they were charging and how much of their annual income came from participation in other similar cases. It seemed like a funny gambit, calling out the fact that the witness had testified in more than three hundred other cases, thinking it might make them less credible and more mercenary, when the same could most certainly be said about their own experts.

The depositions would give her a good introduction to the real world behind the marble columns. For almost her entire life, Jane had an abiding faith in the belief that America, despite its many faults and imperfections, was an inherently just society. Under the Constitution, the most heinous mass murderers were still given the right to a fair trial. Jane saw the perpetrators of the dusty poison in the bottles she used for all those many years as mass murderers of a different kind. How would they try to acquit themselves? What strategies would they employ? How would they profess their blamelessness while looking straight into her eyes?

Jane realized as she filtered through the massive documents how this part of the process was a necessary evil. She had seen enough courtroom television shows to well imagine that part of the judge's job was to cut the fat and keep everything moving at a brisk pace. It was no different from being a teacher in front of a classroom. You didn't want to see your pupils yawning, staring aimlessly out a window, or, worse still, looking at the clock and wishing the hands or the digital display would move faster. So, the deal here was to whittle down what was most important for the courtroom. Most of the material stacked high on her desk would be filed in trolly-like rolling bins, so if anyone involved in the case needed a specific data point from this immense background, it could be easily accessed.

At the same time, Jane knew full well that the defense attorneys were trolling for hidden gold, for anything that might discredit the plaintiff's experts and disqualify their findings in the case. Sowing reasonable doubt in the jury's mind was the clear objective. Did this expert really know what they were talking about? Had they done enough research and published enough peer-reviewed studies to be taken as credible experts? Had they logged the requisite amount of grunt work in their laboratories on exactly this specific kind of case? Were their findings grounded in the most advanced protocols and technologies? How thoroughly did the expert know the company's product? Had they done other cases relating to the same product, and did any of their findings in those prior cases influence their conclusions in this case?

The defense also promoted their positions based on other testing and evaluative approaches that the company had been amassing for decades, including a good portion of the dossier Neal was given when he got the assignment. Ultimately, the outcome of the case would rest almost entirely on conflicting scientific views. Could the witnesses skillfully defend their own state-of-the-art technologies and methodologies against the tried-and-true ones relied upon by the company to demonstrate their innocence? The objective was clearly to downgrade the witnesses' opinions, expertise, and credibility against the long-standing gospel put out by the company and its team of scientists and researchers.

It was not all one-sided. The plaintiff's case was also helped by some newly unearthed and subpoenaed internal corporate documents that flew in the face of their product purity claims. Emily also had the chance to question all the defense experts on this issue, advancing the absurdity of the company's claims of the product being completely safe and harmless. In other words, given the wealth of evidence, how would anyone with an ounce of intelligence fall for that? Jane was particularly impressed with how Emily was so easily able to challenge them on their testing, protocols, and standards, arguing how all were deliberately planned to mask any presence of asbestos fibers in their product.

After she had plowed through the first files, Jane developed her own method of speed-reading since all of the depositions seemed to follow a similar structure. She found a way to breeze through the boring procedural parts and, at times, incomprehensible scientific babble to hone in on what seemed to be most salient. It made her feel like she was back at college studying for final exams, plowing through required course reading. It probably had consumed a whole tree or two to produce the thousands of pages she had read. But what it accomplished was that she would be able to walk into that courtroom in the coming weeks with a good fix on what was going to happen.

When they debriefed after Jane had gone through the last stack of transcripts, Emily was curious to know both her general impressions and any specific questions that might have arisen.

"I do not envy your job." Jane laughed. "I felt a bit overwhelmed at first, trying to digest all of this, but at a certain point, I loosened up and began to relax. In the beginning, it was like I was fish out of water. But as I got further into it, I realized that I didn't need to know all those details. I was getting the gist. I think it was really helpful because it's not quite the alien universe to me anymore. But it still perplexes me how these intelligent and gifted people can sleep well at night while enabling such blatant wrongdoing. I guess it is all about the paycheck."

Chapter 20

As the days turned into weeks counting down to her court date, Jane could not help noticing how the passage of time seemed to go in slow motion. This was hardly the case under normal circumstances when she had a clean bill of health. Back then, it seemed an unescapable fact that the pace of life accelerated with the years. As a child, summer vacations were endless. Now, the next birthday or Christmas arrived in the blink of an eye. Was it really that many years since Bill Clinton had been president?

Perhaps it was the simple fact that daily routines made most days indistinguishable from the others. In the whirlwind of activities and the exercise of responsibilities, there were so few markers beyond the change of seasons and the rituals of holidays that interrupted the turning of an individual's hamster wheels.

For that reason, it required high diligence to reconstruct in her memory all of the past events her case required, given how all the weeks and years had run together in one big jumble. Being able to pinpoint exact events, dates, and times (especially dating back more than thirty years) was certainly a worry for Jane as she had sat for her deposition and now awaited her appearance on the witness stand. For that reason, she was happy that she had a fairly good collection of family photos that had dates and places scribbled on the backsides. She found it quite remarkable how an old photo capturing a fraction of a second could conjure so much memory. She could often recall who had taken the photo, how she had been feeling in that moment, who might have also been over at the house that day, what someone had said to her that made her laugh, the present that another gave to her that day, and so on. Similarly, she had kept all the cancelled checks from Phil's and her joint account for many more years than the IRS recommended, and they could also dust off long-dormant memories. There were also decades of files with all the receipts from household repairs in case they sold the house.

But in the solitude of her deepest thoughts, something more sinister was at play. The passage of time was also being marked in an equally slow deterioration, one that she chose for the time being to keep a closely guarded secret. To Phil and anyone else who saw her on a daily basis, any changes were so minor and subtle as to be barely perceptible. It also didn't help that Jane did everything she could to disguise any appearance of frailty. More than death, her biggest fear was losing her independence, especially becoming a burden to others. It was also a reason why she tried to avoid meeting up with old colleagues who hadn't seen her in a good while.

At constant work in her mind was an internal yardstick. It was as if she were a sprinter keeping a stopwatch on every practice run, only hers was measuring for personal worst. In climbing the stairs in her house or getting in and out of a car, she would gauge if it was progressively harder than it had been the day or the week before. Was her breath more labored? Did she need to slow down or momentarily stop? Was she feeling a pain that was new or had worsened? All of this had the effect of making the hours of the day go by so slowly.

With her doctor, there was no motivation for her to maintain a false façade. Pain management was a matter of increasing importance. And he would see through her attempts to dodge the truth. He needed to know more intimately what was going on with her to make any adjustments to her treatment. Both parties were not in denial. There was nothing he could do that could reverse her condition. Neither was there a trial on a new experimental drug or treatment at his disposal that could slow the inevitable. It was a matter of palliative care, doing what was necessary to give Jane as much quality of life in whatever time she had left.

"Are you handling all this legal stuff all right? Are you up for it?" This was the doctor's way of registering his concern about what was plain as day to him. He didn't need to take her pulse to feel that her energy and vitality had incrementally diminished since their last visit. It was the stage he had seen play out in other patients. No alarm bells were sounding. Had he been asked his opinion then and there, he would have told Jane to scale back her participation in the trial to a bare minimum. But from the way she was describing it, that was a nonstarter.

"I'm going to be there every day," she told him in no uncertain terms. "I want the jury, the judge, the attorneys, and the people who did this to me to look me in the eyes. I want them to know this happened to a real person. I want them to feel like they have a relationship with me from the time we will be spending together. And I want them to know that what happened to me could happen to them or someone they love. I want to be a daily reminder to them that they can do something about it. It's in their hands."

Chapter 21

Jane and Phil arrived at the Los Angeles County courthouse at 8:00 a.m. They passed through the metal detector and walked past the windows where marriage certificates, building permits, and other documents were expedited. They took the elevator to the third floor. The corridor leading to the courtroom was lined with wooden benches. It was like running a gauntlet of caffeinated and stressful-looking people in professional attire, rolling large briefcases on wheels and murmuring in hushed tones to their clients. Two hundred and fifty feet later, they were at the door marked "Department U, Superior Court Judge Teresa Sanchez." Emily was already there, chatting with someone Jane assumed was one of the opposing counsels, but it was not anyone she immediately recognized from her deposition.

"How are you feeling?"

Jane cracked a strained smile to her attorney before answering. "I'm just glad to be getting this thing underway." Her nervousness had the emotional footprint from her days as a teacher, just like the first day of a new school year, meeting new students for the first time. Her pupils, of course, were always the far more anxious party, checking out this new teacher and hoping to not dread what the next twenty weeks in her classroom might have in store. Once her cover of anonymity would be blown in the coming days, she wanted to make a solid and unambiguous first impression when she took the witness stand, exerting authority and establishing accountability from the first breath, with the honest warmth, curiosity, and openness that were true to her nature.

A few seconds later, a bailiff dressed in a sheriff's uniform opened the door to the courtroom and beckoned those gathered in the immediate proximity to enter. There was nothing in that environment that clashed with her expectations from all the courtrooms she had seen in movies and TV shows. The judge's bench was on a pedestal, clothed in beautiful, dark hardwood, framing the seal of the county of Los Angeles on the wall behind. The jury area was cordoned off to the side as customary.

Jane and Phil took their seats toward the back row near the exit, a safeguard in case she started feeling ill or weak and wanted to leave early without calling attention to herself. It all conformed to the common practice for plaintiffs in civil cases to not sit together with their attorneys, as they would in criminal cases.

Emily had spared Jane the ordeal of sitting through several prior court days taken up with pretrial motions and all the nuts and bolts to ensure the integrity of a smooth-running trial.

From her perch in the back, Jane studied the jury box in some detail, both in wide angle to see the group as a whole and then darting her attention to random members who caught her eye. At that moment and without being totally conscious of it, Jane reacted as both the student and the teacher. The jury members were like her students. Although she was for the moment just another face in the back, she would soon become the center of their attention, the sole reason why their normal lives were being interrupted for the duration, whether welcomed or not. Like her students, they were compelled to be there as their civic duty and had to behave according to specific rules of decorum and dress code (no wifebeaters, no open-toed shoes or flip-flops).

Like her students, they would all form their first takes about her when she took the witness stand in the next day or two. Would she seem likable, credible, secure, and self-confident? Or would they see her as fearful, anxious, feeble, and sickly? God forbid she should keel over in the courtroom! At the same point, she was also the student. Her performance, not only in her testimony but also how she held up in her seat in the gallery, would be judged and graded by the people in the box.

After completing her scan, Jane thought the twelve jurors looked no different from the people she might encounter in line at the supermarket. They were every shape and size. Ages ranged, from her best estimate, from late twenties to seventies. They were evenly split, six men and six women. There were two Hispanics, one African American, two Asians, and seven Caucasians. There were also alternate jurors seated, whom she would find out about in greater detail later in the proceedings.

A door opened, and out came a graying, darkhaired woman in her late fifties, attired in a black gown. The bailiff asked that all present rise from their seats as the judge took her seat and then asked everyone except the jury to be seated. The bailiff then swore in the prospective jury members before they, too, took their seats.

The judge formally welcomed everyone, gave the jury instructions, and asked the legal teams to introduce themselves. As she was listening, Jane felt a shockwave of anxiety that prompted her to take two deep breaths, as painful as it was to fill her lungs to capacity. Emily glanced back with a worried look on her brow. Jane gestured back with an assuring slight wave of her hand, as though her outstretched fingers were comforting a crying child.

Jane talked herself down in those few seconds, believing that feeling that way in that moment was entirely natural. Again, being the teacher gave her a perspective that was the raw material of nightmares, the kind where she might suddenly discover that she was standing totally naked in front of her young students. It was the consideration that there was a body of coursework she had mastered and needed to find the best way to explain it in age-appropriate, bite-sized chunks so their young minds could digest it. What she imagined happening in this courtroom could be a hundred times worse.

In her conversation with Emily after reading through the depositions, Jane expressed her concern about the utter complexity of her case. As a teacher, part of the job was to not overwhelm her students. She couldn't help wondering how in the hell the material she had combed through would be understandable to the twelve men and women who would decide the case. It felt like asking a middle schooler to write a doctoral thesis. Even the judge would need to have the knowledge of an MD, PhD, and MBA to know authoritatively what half of the witnesses were talking about. The case relied on data seen through electron microscopes and other intolerably complex technical explanations of testing methods and lab results, plus an insider's knowledge of business philosophy and practices.

"It seems like there is so much splitting of hairs and so much incomprehensible techno-babble. Who's going to believe who?" Jane had asked her attorney.

"You'll see," Emily reassured her. "Take my word for it. There's a method to the madness. Both sides have been through this dozens of times. We know where the tipping factors are, and we go right to the core. There's a way to simplify it without insulting everyone's intelligence. It's a careful balancing act to give just enough information so the jury takes away just what they need to make a reasonable, informed decision."

"I can see from all your happy faces that you're all very excited about jury service and couldn't wait to get here this morning," the judge joked as she began the jury instructions. She asked for a show of hands on how many had served on a jury before, then separately if they had serviced on criminal versus civil cases. She then took the time to make sure the jury fully understood the difference. "In criminal cases, we talk about 'beyond a reasonable doubt.' That means an abiding conviction of the truth of the charges. Here, instead, we are talking about 'preponderance of the evidence,' which is not as high a burden of proof. It means 'more likely than not.' It's still a burden, and if you conclude that it's balanced fifty-fifty, then the plaintiff's attorneys have not done their job." The jurors also were told that this case did not require a unanimous decision like in criminal trials, but only nine out of twelve. She also admonished them not to talk to any of the attorneys or any of the witnesses in the hallways or otherwise. "They'd love to talk to you. But if you see them in the street, you are not allowed to even say, 'Hi. How are you?'" She also told them that the only evidence they were to consider was what was presented in the witness stand. Anything that the lawyers said was not evidence. Lastly, they were admonished not to discuss the case outside the jury room.

Before they adjourned for a brief break, the attorneys stood up and introduced themselves to the jury. They told them who they represented and read out the list of witnesses and experts they planned to call. When

Emily made her presentation, the first person on that witness list was Jane. After giving them a brief summary of the case they were about to hear, the judge then asked if the jury knew any of the people mentioned on the lists or had any connection whatsoever to their enterprises. They were also questioned if they had any experience with asbestos-related issues or if their work experience gave them any special expertise that might prejudice their consideration of the evidence. The judge emphasized that the trial would probably last fifteen days, wanting to make sure that none of the jury members had extenuating circumstances such as extreme financial hardship. Two of the jurors begged off and were replaced by alternate jurors. After the grilling was over, all had affirmed that they could be fair and impartial.

When they had returned from the break, the attorneys had the opportunity to excuse members of the jury without stating a cause if they believed that juror might have beliefs that would not serve their clients. Exercising this peremptory challenge, four of the jurors were excused, mostly at the defense's request. New prospective jurors were seated, and the process of interviewing them continued anew until both attorneys ultimately accepted the panel as it was. As the tedious process dragged on, Jane grew more exhausted and uncomfortable, so Phil and she quietly escaped through the nearby doors to rest up for the next day.

Chapter 22

Jane and Phil were at the courthouse for the start of the next day's session. She had made a promise both to Emily and to herself that she would be present every day unless it proved to be physically impossible. She learned the day before that it wasn't as clear cut as all that. She was clearly not in command any longer. The disease was now dictating the shots. There were thankfully days when she could go about her business largely untinged by her condition. But she realized it was all highly unpredictable. She might wake up and feel emboldened to take on the world after a cup of coffee, only to just as suddenly run out of gas. Without warning, her seat in the courtroom might become unbearably hard and torturous to sit in. Furthermore, her mental acuity, which had never been in question before, seemed to ebb and flow with increasing volatility. The suddenness had been apparent yesterday. Moments before, she had felt good enough and confident enough to last for the whole session, only to feel that she couldn't abide it for another second. She hoped for a better outcome today, especially since it was more likely than not that she would be called to the witness stand.

Before that could happen, she would have to make it through the opening statements from both sides. And prior to that, the judge went through a more detailed set of jury instructions. Jane was fascinated and somewhat aghast at how the judge systematically ran through all the convoluted ways the same information could be heard differently through a maze of complicated filters we all possess.

The judge hoped with this little talk that the jurors would become fairer and more adept. For example, she pointed out how they should not be influenced if one side had more witnesses than the other. Or what to do if they thought that one thing a witness said was untrue; should that color their opinion about the rest of the testimony if the other statements seemed credible? Easier said than done, they would need to find a way to park their biases, stereotypes, perceptions, and other prejudices outside the door. "Your verdict must be based solely on the evidence presented. You must carefully evaluate the evidence and resist any urge to reach a verdict that is influenced by bias for or against any party or witness."

As the judge spoke, Jane thought back to a classic film she saw during her college days, Kurosawa's *Rashomon*. At the beginning of the film, everyone knows that horrendous crimes have been committed, a killing and a rape. The rest of the film consists of four significantly different versions of what happened, told by firsthand witnesses, each one more plausible and believable than the other. There was a lot of subjectivity in her story as well, assumptions that seemed plausible, the connecting of dots that relied on logical outcomes. The other side was no doubt going to be equally skillful at making their case. The very thought gave Jane a sour taste in the pit of her stomach.

The need for the judge's admonishing talk became more self-evident as the opening statements began. The intention of the lawyers in their preambles was that this was clearly an open-and-shut case favoring their respective side. Wearing her teacher's hat again, Jane was listening with curiosity about how the attorneys spoke to the jury. None of the jury members to her recollection were overly educated, to put it mildly, from their background profiles. The ones with the fancy degrees (and therefore too smart for their own good in the defense counsel's opinion) had been whittled away. What was left was a mix of people working in white- and blue-collar jobs that required a fair modicum of intelligence and competency but firmly in a respectable but totally average way.

Emily stood and addressed the jury and wasted no time in introducing Jane to them, pointing to her at her seat so there would be no mistaken identity. As if watching a tennis match, all the members in the box turned their heads in unison to fix on Jane. Jane met their gaze, feeling how each one of them was in effect undressing her, checking for any visible signs of decrepitude. On Jane's side, this was the end of her anonymity, of blending into the background. From now on, she would be on everyone's radar. Her body language, her gestures, even a yawn would hardly escape notice or scrutiny.

I know what they are all thinking right now, Jane thought, cracking a little smile at her self-amusement. *"It sure sucks to be you!"*

Emily began what amounted to a one-on-one conversation with the jury, giving the effect that the rest of the assembled audience was frozen in suspended animation. Without overembellishing, Emily injected an emotional intensity into her tone, designed to give each listener an immediacy. In telling the story of Jane's life, Emily wanted to leave room for each juror to make their own connection via Jane, linking to a feeling reminding them of someone they perhaps loved, cared for, and admired in their own family—maybe someone who may have died under similar circumstances. If anything, she did all she could to bring out the humanity of Jane, not in just celebrating awards and accomplishments but highlighting the kindness and goodness in her heart that had so positively impacted the lives of so many.

A picture is worth a thousand words, and the photos Jane had gone through in her deposition were flashed on a large video screen for all to see. There was almost a silent collective sigh as the jury saw the pictures of Jane in good health and radiating vitality. The woman they now spied in the back row by the door was quite literally a pale imitation. It was easy to imagine that her life force had sprung a leak, and day by day, it only became worse. There were wrinkles and hollowed cheekbones and stringy, limp hair that never totally regained its body and sheen from the assault of chemotherapy and heavy medicines. All that remained in front of them was a shell of a person, who was clearly marshalling all her energy to be with them there that day.

Emily detailed what the eye could not see, the scars and the various diseased organs that were cut from her body and discarded as medical waste. What was harder to describe in words was the searing pain that Jane had to endure through all her procedures and treatments, all the way up to the present moment. Before she finished that portion of her presentation, the listeners had a fair idea of what it would feel like to be on the inside of Jane's body. It brought home to them a recognition of all the things they took for granted that had become for Jane matters of enormous struggle to just get through the simplest activities in her life.

Once all possible human compassion was milked out of the audience in talking about Jane, the warm and fuzzy tone evaporated into a logical and linear presentation of the cold, science-based, hard facts. Emily gave a preview of what she hoped the evidence would conclusively demonstrate. She spoke of the century-long history of the corporation and more specifically of the talc that was one of their signature products. She spoke of the generations who trusted this product and had no idea that it was tainted with asbestos. She told of the documentary evidence that would come forward that the company was aware of this problem and did everything to keep it secret. Worse yet, they purposefully used inadequate testing methods and rubber stamp trade associations to bolster their bogus product purity claims.

Emily hammered this point home. "By the 1970s (and even by the late 60s), there is no question that there was information out there for any company that was using talc, that they should be concerned that the talc they were using was contaminated with asbestos. There was information at their fingertips if they wanted it. The evidence will show that the company knew about these hazards and should have done something about it."

Strikingly, Emily held up a common thimble used in sewing and told the jury how two billion asbestos fibers could fit inside of it. That statistic was even more damning when she described the scope of exposure Jane had from daily use throughout most of her lifetime. Her mother had used it on herself and on Jane and her siblings as babies. Her use intensified as she entered puberty and continued unabated for decades.

"Each and every day that she used it, she would apply it the same way," Emily explained. "It was a dust. It was a powder. It smelled good. She put it all over her body. And on each of those occasions, she breathed the dust that was generated from the natural use of that product. Each and every time she used it, she was exposed to asbestos."

Before closing, Emily gave a brief overview of the key facts about asbestos, what it looked like and what kinds were commonly found in the talc that caused mesothelioma. She elaborated again for emphasis on how the corporation used testing technology that was incapable of detecting asbestos, much to the verbal objections of the opposing counsel. In response, Emily forgot momentarily about the jury, launching into a detailed technical discourse about the company's testing technology that turned them glossy-eyed. She gave them notice about the experts she would be calling in the coming days and what pieces of the evidentiary puzzle they would be adding.

When the brief recess was over, it was the defense's turn to make their opening statement. Jane sunk back in her seat and tried to get as comfortable as possible for what she imagined would be another very long-winded presentation. What was a bit unwelcomed on her side was the attention the opposing attorney lavished on her. Robert, the slightly overweight and balding lawyer for the corporation, was an accomplished actor in Jane's view. It took someone of that skill to walk the very fine line between being sympathetic and empathetic of the wreck that she had become, while not coming off as a cruel and heartless standard-bearer for a greedy and ruthless corporate behemoth.

In contrast to Emily's presentation, Robert's audience was the jury plus one—Jane. The last thing he wanted to do was add fuel to the fire of the heavy emotional context concerning Jane and the horrible disease called mesothelioma that was killing her right before everyone's eyes. So, he went out of his way to heap praise on Jane as a wonderful human being and to bemoan her terrible fate. "No one deserves to get a terminal disease." In his next breath, he also spoke highly of Emily as a great attorney who would be doing a skillful job on behalf of her client. "It doesn't mean that we agree on much." And the biggest point of disagreement, he quickly added, was the notion that his client had any responsibility whatsoever for the cause of Jane's disease. "We dispute that her disease has anything to do with our product." The acting job was in full gear to personify "the good people of the corporation" also as an aggrieved party, victimized as well by what the evidence would demonstrate were baseless accusations.

Jane was having a problem hiding her consternation at Robert's uncategorical denial that the company's talc products had even a trace of asbestos and his insistence that the claims to the contrary were based on outmoded and discredited technologies. He rattled off the names of a number of scientists who would be verifying the company's data. He cited some others who had published papers identifying asbestos in talc that they later recanted because of advancements in scientific methods. He gave the impressive-sounding credentials of the experts he would be calling to counter Emily's witnesses.

He spoke of the purity of the mines that had provided the talc and how exhaustive the testing of the raw materials by the labs was, well regarded and trusted by US government health agencies. He asked the jury to consider the fact that the miners in Italy who had exposures to talc dust "hundreds of thousands of times" more severe than Jane's had zero mesothelioma cases according to a long-term epidemiological research study.

Robert wanted the jury to consider that talc is one of the most widely used mineral products in our daily life. He told of one expert who they would hear from who would tell them how we are literally engulfed in asbestos. "Asbestos is a naturally occurring mineral. It exists throughout the state of California. So just by virtue of the winds coming off the hills, yeah, certainly a lot of it had been used in products and used in and around shipyards in the Bay Area, Long Beach, and San Diego. But we have asbestos in the air we breathe." He spoke of another expert who would talk about how all of us have an abundance of asbestos fibers in our bodies by virtue of living in these urban areas. "But just because we breathe all this asbestos doesn't mean that we're all at risk to get an asbestos-related disease." He said this expert would speak to this "ambient or background exposure." In fact, the testimony would bear out that Jane's exposure to asbestos, even if it were in the talc, would have been so minute on its own to cause mesothelioma.

The judge interrupted Robert to request that they take a lunch break. When they returned, Emily approached the bench for a conference with the judge and Robert. She reported that Jane was requesting to postpone her testimony until the next day. The proceedings had been more exhausting than she had reckoned, and she had to go home. The judge agreed, and Robert concluded his opening remarks quickly, making perhaps his most striking claim that it was not even certain that Jane's mesothelioma was conclusively caused by asbestos. He told the jury that the medical experts would explain all of this in due course.

On the way home, Jane told Phil that she didn't know if she was going to be able to see this process through. "I just didn't think that it would be this demoralizing, and this is just the beginning."

You don't have to worry," Phil assured her. "Even if you never show up again, Emily has what she needs. Remember, they have your video deposition. There's absolutely no pressure on you. It's totally up to you."

Chapter 23

One of the unpleasant things Neal noticed about his own aging process was that he was becoming more and more brittle with each passing year. It was something that was an inescapable reality felt whenever he was out on the golf course. Swinging his driver over his shoulder to harness the maximum thrust to impact the ball on the tee was not the effortless, fluid movement of before. Reaching the apex of his motion, he could feel an unpleasant and unnerving tension at the stretching of the ligaments and tendons attaching his shoulders to his arms. The beauty of the sport for him had always been the seamless merging of the physical and mental that brought him a temporary spiritual uplifting. His worldly concerns evaporated at that moment of contact as he watched the trajectory of the little white ball on its path down the fairway.

Suddenly, this enjoyment was coupled with an encroaching sense of fear and dread. Like a rubber band that had been pulled and stretched to its limit and had begun to fray, he felt that each swing brought him closer to a finality, perhaps surgery and/or an involuntary retirement from the game. He also noticed how the aches and pains of being a weekend warrior had intensified in severity and duration. The warranty on his resiliency was expiring.

The same could be said of Neal's capacity to deal with the stress and strains on the job. Unpleasant things that he might have brushed off in the past or expedited with equal effortless aplomb to his tee shots were becoming increasingly taxing. In his younger days, he looked at his older superiors with an illusion that they were revered village elders there to dispense their sage wisdom to the younger warriors. Now, he was one of the elders, but that old politburo he had looked up to was sadly nowhere to be found. In its place were analytics and spreadsheets, financial and investor projections, and market trend analyses that couldn't give a squat about what the brand did a generation before to solve a similar problem. Decades-long experience was no longer revered but patronizingly acknowledged with a pat on the back.

Instead of being in his corner office and consulted on the major big-picture issues, Neal was feeling like a fish out of water in the transition between the old conventional ways and the new order. The rules had suddenly changed, with an abruptness that demanded flexibility. Old dogs needed to quickly learn new tricks. The only problem now was Neal was getting fatigued. His brain muscles were not that flexible either.

Neal was whining to himself as he opened a large file that he had deliberately ignored for the last few days in his briefcase. Inside was a printout of a briefing on Jane's case. Every job, even at the senior executive level, had undesirable and unfulfilling aspects that came with the turf. It was like a child having to eat his vegetables in order to get dessert. Do you get it done and out of the way quickly, or do you hold off until the last possible moment? Neal had chosen the latter. As he began to peruse the contents, Neal's anger was centered on the question of if his old boss would have been tasked with what was considered to be grunt work.

He already knew that Jane's case was categorized as highly sensitive to the company. And it wasn't the first time he had been charged with representing the company in court. Thankfully, in the majority of the cases, someone lower on the pecking order was called upon, especially if the location was not in a major media market and the case was not as potentially toxic. But this was a time when having the longevity with the company and being in such a senior position brought an advantage of credibility. Being a relic of a bygone time was suddenly an asset rather than a millstone.

Neal was loath to admit it to himself, but he detested everything about being a party to these cases. On the most superficial level, there was no allure to traveling even with first-class airfare and accommodations. He greatly preferred being at home with his wife and dog. His bucket list of places to go and explore was already pretty much checked off. But that was only the start.

At the top of that list was how this was an exercise in just about everything that Neal hated about modern society. "We have become a country of victims," he complained to some of the lawyers briefing him on a previous case. "I heard that Starbucks had to put a warning on their cups because someone sued them because they had spilled their coffee and burned themselves." Living life was a liability. Shit happened. Why did it always have to be someone else's fault? What happened to personal responsibility? Or were all bets off when there was a lawyer and an opportunity to cash in?

He thought about airplane manufacturers and airlines that had to deal with the aftermath of plane crashes. Yes, it was dangerous to fly, but it was statistically safer than getting in the car. The benefits of rapid transportation far outweighed the microscopic risk of dying in a crash. Similarly, millions of people had used the company's products, including the talcum powder, for generations without much apparent harm and with great benefit; otherwise, they would not have been so popular for so long. Suddenly, it was now the stuff of television commercials. There were big bucks to be made. It was open season, with his company in the crosshairs.

As he leafed through the paperwork, there was nothing much that deviated from the last case where he had testified. There was a fact sheet and photo of Jane. There was a summary of her medical history, followed by the details of her purported use of the company's products throughout the years. The rest would best be described as a script, detailing in bullet form the company's position and arguments in support of their innocence. The attorneys had enough experience under their belt to anticipate almost every possible question that the opposition might throw at them. So, Neal needed to master these points and recite them back in a natural and convincing manner. There was even a brief primer (probably added by the corporate psychologist) on how to behave around plaintiffs, should he encounter them in the courtroom. Nothing was left to chance.

His flight to Los Angeles was booked to depart in two days.

Chapter 24

Emily took matters into her own hands when she saw Jane leave the courtroom early for a second day in a row. During a brief recess later that afternoon, she called Phil to tell him that she wanted to put off Jane's testimony, at least for the next few days. She had made the mistake early on in her career, against her better judgment, of allowing a client to testify who was clearly in a compromised condition.

Jane was not happy about it since she had prepared herself mentally for the upcoming ordeal, but deep inside, she was relieved. As she had sat in the courtroom, she became acutely aware of her symptoms, which grew worse as the clock wore on. She had taken the lowest recommended therapeutic dose of an opioid painkiller as a precaution to at least give the appearance of comfort and clarity. But it was clearly not enough. Each difficult breath she took in her one remaining lung seemed insufficient to provide her with the oxygen she needed. Every inhale felt like small daggers were stabbing her. She had remembered times when she was forced to go to work and teach when she had a bug, and how difficult it was to hold herself together, pumping herself full of aspirins and antihistamines. In her mind, this was a hundred times worse. Maybe a million times.

"Let her have a couple of days to rest up, and then let's reevaluate," Emily advised. Before the session ended that day, Emily asked for a sidebar with the judge and Robert to let them know about the change. The testimony of other witnesses would have to be moved up to compensate, and Robert would have to give his consent that he would be likewise prepared. "In the worst case, we have Jane testify toward the end if she is up to it," Emily proposed. "Barring that, we can show the video of her deposition."

Perhaps it was all for the best for her overall mental state that Jane was skipping the next days. What all the testimony amounted to was a crash course for the jury about mesothelioma and asbestos so they would have as close to an informed basis as possible when it came time to render a verdict. Sitting through all that was certainly a degree of detail that she didn't need at this point. She would have walked away with a greater scientific understanding of the physiology, chemistry, pathology, and diagnostic technologies of her condition. There was no doubt about that. She had already had a taste of that when plowing through the deposition transcripts. Whether enduring all this trial testimony would have ultimately been of any real importance to her was highly unlikely. She was already living with the repercussions of this terrible disease. There was nothing she would hear that would alter that reality. By sitting out, she probably spared herself some highly disturbing and demoralizing thoughts. "With all of this accrued knowledge, how could they have let this happen to me and thousands of others?"

"If something significant happens, any surprises, I will fill you both in," Emily assured Phil. She reiterated, however, that this first phase usually went according to a fairly predictable playbook.

The first experts who appeared were there to confirm without a shadow of a doubt all the scientific reasons why there was a case to begin with. They would all be asked to basically summarize their curriculum vitae, listing all their degrees, giving the names and dates of all the institutions of higher learning they attended. Their particular areas of research and study were detailed, and any relevant publications they had authored were all served up and scrutinized. Lastly, they were asked about their current places of work and affiliations, with special emphasis on work that would qualify them as credible experts on the matters in question.

Upon cross-examination, the defense would try to promote doubt in the jury's mind. Were these people just guns for hire who manipulated the data to bias the conclusions their clients wanted to hear? Just how mercenary were they? The would ask not only how much they were being paid for their work on this trial but also what they earned doing this gig on an annual basis. More fundamentally, was all their work in this field really relevant to the individual circumstances at stake in this case? Were their testing and diagnostic technologies all they were cracked up to be? How credibly would they defend their findings when presented with opposing views from experts with equally lofty CVs? Were they knocked off guard or did they appear overly defensive when their work was criticized or debunked? Or did they stand their ground and respond in a confident and sensible way?

Through all of it, the judge was there in a motherly way to make sure the jury was not bulldozed by the onslaught. Had Jane been there, she would have shared the jury's relief that the judge was holding a tight rein on the lawyers, so they were not transgressing into the kind of inflammatory oratory designed to inappropriately sway their emotions. The judge was also vigilant to make sure all the ground rules agreed upon during the pretrial motions and planning, designed to keep them focused and on track, were adhered to diligently by both sides.

All of the experts who appeared that first day that Jane missed had one thing in common. Each saw the biology and chemistry of the world around them through a particular tinted lens. For example, the material scientist who testified that day saw his universe as an expression of molecules and crystals through his electron microscope that might be fifty thousand times smaller than what we could detect with the naked eye.

The jury had watched Jane as she left the courtroom early the day before, so they did not need an expert to tell them that she was damaged. They didn't need a doctor's note to prove that she was in horrible shape. But they learned something very quickly that next day: whether or not they would find culpability and award damages in this case rested not on what they could see with their eyes but in the exacting interpretation of those tiniest of particles. Each expert brought their own piece of the puzzle. Those particles would be measured in the air, in the container of the product, and inside Jane's tissues. It would all come down to the one scientist's word against another.

Chapter 25

While Jane convalesced at home, the jury room coffee maker was at full throttle. It was needed to stay alert during the hours-long onslaught of convoluted scientific explanations and terminology. As a teacher, Jane knew all too well the telltale signs of losing her audience when course material went over her students' heads. Their eyeballs, which had for the most part been focused on her, would suddenly drift upward toward the ceiling. They might be asking themselves the fundamental *What in the hell is she talking about?* question. Or worse still, *What in the hell am I doing wasting my time here?* The jury members were each challenged to keep up appearances, stifling any yawns or other fidgety signs of incomprehension or boredom. This was a serious matter laden with responsibility, and they had promised to do their duty. Caffeine helped but only up to a certain point.

The attorneys on both sides and the witnesses who were there to explain the scientific foundation of the case had a major advantage over everyone else in the courtroom. They were experienced and were working off a well-formulated playbook. As much as the experts tried to dummy down their explanations to something a layperson might understand, it could all disappear in the heartbeat. Once under attack during cross-examination, the gloves usually came off as professional integrity was called into question. It could degenerate into serious wonkdom.

At those moments, the witness and the attorneys might as well have been speaking a foreign language. Maybe someone should have thought to provide the jury with a pocket-sized glossary. TEM grids, NIOSH protocols, PCME (phase contrast microscopy equivalents), the difference between the 7400 and 7402 methods, the PLM and the PCM analyses—it was all mumbo jumbo. Explaining a millimeter to people not on the metric system was a challenge by itself: "A millimeter is 1/1000 of a meter," expounded one expert. "Another way to look at it: if you wear glasses and you put your fingers over them and still see some light between the tips of your fingers, that's a millimeter." Interspersed with all of this was the distraction of the constant interruption of objections.

Each member of the jury had to come up with his or her individualized survival plans. How much of all of this could they or should they intellectually absorb? Was it good enough to just barely get the overall gist? Lacking the perspective of the experts, the jury could have trouble weighing the respective merits of one parcel of information over the next. To circumvent overwhelm, some of the jury members secretly practiced selective inattention. Some who might have been more astute at reading the energy of personalities used that as their gauge. When the intensity of the moment made the needle go into the red zone, they might perk up from their masked stupor and put the info into the priority file of their memory. So, as much as the attorneys were engaged in a high-stakes game, the twelve people in the box invented their own game as well to prevent their brains from self-immolating.

Another dance that happened every time an expert witness took the stand was a rather extensive, detailed, and snooze-worthy presentation of the person's qualifications. Whether they were testifying for the plaintiff or the defense, no stone would be left unturned talking about their education, the universities they attended, the topics they mastered, the gurus they studied under, the research they completed, and so on. Then they would go through the same drill about their career after completing school, the institutions and noted experts they worked for, their fancy titles, the research projects they were part of, the number of peer-reviewed articles in prestigious journals they had coauthored, hopefully narrowing in on the very reason why their opinion in this case should be taken as the last word. Of course, the opposition would then devote a lot of energy to shoot holes into the witness's integrity, portraying the expert as a money-grubbing whore, moving from one case to another, manipulating their opinions and shoehorning their data to satisfy their paying clients.

The first witness was the original pathologist working at the hospital who initially processed Jane's tissue samples and made the diagnosis of both her ovarian cancer and the mesothelioma. It was to establish with no uncertainty the scientific basis for why this matter was before the court. During Emily's questioning, the doctor explained in detail the extent and magnitude of each occurrence, where the tumors were specifically located and to what degree the cancer had spread to lymph nodes and other organs and tissues.

The jury got its first display of defense tactics during cross-examination designed to degrade and discredit the plaintiff's claims. There was no smoking gun in what this doctor was presenting, and there was no intention from the outset that it should. That was to come later, but the jury knew nothing of that at the time. This was just the first layer, documenting the beginning of Jane's descent.

What Robert wanted to accomplish during his cross-examination was to seed doubt in the jury's mind. The witness had not done any advanced examination of Jane's tissues that shed any light on whether there was any trace to be found of the powder (and asbestos fibers) she used for decades. All the witness had done was to identify the cancers and render the diagnoses. Robert also wanted to subvert the witness to testify to facts that might substantiate in part their claims of innocence.

"If the talcum powder that was actually owned or actually used by Jane did not contain asbestos, you would not consider her use of that product to be a substantial contributing cause of the disease; correct?"

"That is correct."

"Your expert report does not say expressly, but is it fair to me to assume, by omission, that you found no pulmonary markers of asbestos exposure?"

"Correct. If I did, it would be one of the diagnoses."

"And there were no asbestos fibers or asbestos bodies in her lung or lymph node tissue, to your knowledge."

"None of these tissues were biopsied by me for that purpose. So, there's no information in terms of whether there are any asbestos fibers or asbestos bodies either in the lungs or in the lymph nodes."

"And would the same be true for her abdominal and pelvic cavities?"

"In my pathology reports, there was no mention of asbestos fibers or asbestos bodies being identified in the tissue."

"With respect to evidence of talc use, you found no pulmonary markers of talc exposure either. Correct? No talcosis. No talc particles. And no evidence of talc particles found in her abdominal or pelvic cavities. Correct?"

"Not that I know of. However, it is well known that the talc disappears at a rapid rate, and the relatively smaller fibers are much less likely to form asbestos bodies and too small to see as just fibers by light microscopy."

"With respect to the laundry list of abnormalities I have mentioned, you're not offering the opinion, to a reasonable degree of medical certainty, that they were caused by asbestos exposure. Correct?"

"That is not correct."

The doctor explained his answer by describing asbestos exposure as the undoubtable cause of her mesothelioma and went on to explain the common link between the two separate cancers.

Robert postulated other potential causes of her disorders, including trauma from her surgeries and complications from chemotherapy. Could she have had genetic defects or blood factors that could have caused her problems, and why wasn't she tested for these?

The sparring continued for the next hour. Did the witness have improper consultation with the plaintiff? Did the doctor have a command of all the current and past literature on the topic, and did he follow all standard testing methods, protocols, and regulations? The witness held his own under the barrage. Robert could only hope his tactics had begun the process of chipping away at that "more likely than not" burden of proof the judge had mentioned in the jury instructions.

Chapter 26

What the jury panelists soon realized a short while into the testimony of the second witness was that they had been given a relatively gentle baptism by fire into what was now developing into hand-to-hand combat between the two sides. While still cloaked in professional decorum, the tension was ratcheting up. In the boundary between reality and fiction, the truth often lay shrouded in an area of the grayest murkiness. The experts testifying before them had raised their hands to swear an oath. The attorneys and the experts each side had hired would make convincing arguments that their version of the story was the truth. They compiled documentation in support so there would be substance behind their words. But one thing was for certain as the jury began soaking in all the rhetoric. Both sides could not be telling the whole truth. One of the parties had to be lying, repeating falsehoods so often so they had taken on the appearance of truth, stretching credulity to its outer limit.

There was one assumption none of the parties would dispute. The company would not have deliberately added asbestos as an ingredient in its talc-based products. None of the benefits of the industrial uses of the fibers, like those in auto parts, home-improvement products, or heating systems, applied here. So, after establishing that Jane was sick with a disease caused only by asbestos, Emily needed to present conclusive proof of how the asbestos got into the product in the first place.

The mineralogist hired by the plaintiff gave an exhaustive overview of everything anybody would need to know about asbestos fibers. He took them back in time to address how talc deposits were formed when the earth's crust solidified, breaking it down into the various chemical compounds, composed of magnesium silicate talc, aluminum silicates, and silica oxide. He spoke about the different forms of asbestos naturally found in talc and their individual characteristics, showing pictures of how to readily distinguish between the anthrophyllite, tremolite, and chrysotile types. He asked them to pay particular note to the shape of the cylindrical asbestos fibers, measuring at a ratio of eight to ten times longer in length than width.

There was much for the jury to decipher about the various technologies and techniques used in the process of positively identifying asbestos in the raw material. There was good reason why Emily went into this is such exhaustive detail and Robert spent so much effort to counter. It would be safe to say that most on the jury only knew of the kind of microscopes they might have looked through in a high school biology class, simply called a stereo or standard-type light microscope. Looking at an asbestos fiber on a slide with this microscope, the information would be quite limited to the largest of fibers and bundles of fibers down to about one micron. Now, they were hearing in detail about electron microscopes of various types, capable of seeing images as much as ten thousand times smaller.

First, they learned about scanning electron microscopy. It uses a beam of electrons that illuminates much more powerfully than a beam of light. It requires a power supply of as much as 40,000 kilovolts to generate that beam, compared to 120 volts used in our households or with light microscopes. In case of the scanning electron microscope, the image is formed by the electrons that interact with the fiber or specimen and the electron released from the specimen at individual points as a result of this interaction. It is measured based on electric current as the specimen is very rapidly swept across or scanned. With the transmission electron microscope (TEM), the electron beam either is stopped or passes through the sample, forming an image similar to what is generated by an x-ray of a broken arm. With magnification up to 250,000 times, the mineralogist gets a lot of information about the morphology or overall structure of the specimens or fibers. With both SEM and TEM, one can use an accessory that determines the elemental composition and ratio by the x-ray energy released by the interaction of the electron with the fiber or specimen, called energy dispersive spectroscopy (EDS). But that would still not be specific enough to testify in court with all certainty, confirming the presence of asbestos.

What was needed was an even more specific analysis called SAED (selected area electron diffraction) using the TEM. It was the only absolute way to confirm the identity of an asbestos fiber. It literally caused electrons to diffract off the fiber in a specific pattern that by measuring the spacing between lines of dots and lines and determining the angle created, it reveals the inherent crystalline structure. The pattern of dots given off would be unique to a chrysotile fiber compared to any other, such as an anthophyllite or tremolite. All in all, the mineralogist would claim to be on solid ground if they could confirm three elements: 1) it looked like a fiber; 2) its chemistry matched the known reference materials for that fiber; and 3) it had the precise crystal structure confirmed to be unique to that fiber.

The mineralogist gave his findings that the samples he tested from three known suppliers of raw talc to the company from mines in Italy, Vermont, and Montana. They tested positive for the presence of chrysotile, tremolite, and anthophyllite type asbestos. The most common forms found in cosmetic products are tremolite and anthophyllite type asbestos and the type of fiber identified as the primary agent of Jane's mesothelioma.

When it was his turn to cross-examine the mineralogist, Robert was ready with his counterarguments. There was nothing that caught him off guard. As authoritative as the mineralogist spoke, Robert's job was to present a trove of ambiguities to water it down. Just as the plaintiff's side followed a very logical presentation, Robert's questioning was equally thorough and deliberate, based on patterns well established from earlier trials.

By this time, the jury was not surprised by any effort to question the mineralogist's qualifications and biases. How much was he getting paid for this trial? Did test findings that he had processed for other clients at other trials influence his opinions here? Had he testified exclusively for plaintiffs? (This became a moot point when he answered that he had served in similar roles for both sides.) Was there any daylight to be found in the scientific protocols and data points he used compared to generally accepted industrial standards found in the original research?

As Robert peppered the expert with questions, some on the jury flashed back on unpleasant memories of pop quizzes in school and the embarrassment they had felt at falling flat. Could the samples he processed have been contaminated in the testing laboratory by asbestos in the air or dust on the counters or corridors (a sentiment those prone to conspiracy theories would love)? He answered that the only known source for such contamination would historically be from any kind of construction at the lab or contamination from other specimens and not a factor in the timing of this work. Was his measuring of the data and, more specifically, his instruments correctly calibrated and tested to eliminate potential false readings?

The purposeful mission with this line of questioning was to suggest that there were many possibilities for error, concluding that the mineralogist's findings could not be considered absolute. Of course, the jury would soon be hearing from a counterpart hired by the corporation who would bring an opposing view.

Before he finished, Robert saved his biggest salvo to defuse the testimony by raising doubt about the science of identification of the fibers itself. There was one loophole about the very structure of the fibers, those considered to be asbestiform or nonasbestiform. Both fiber types had a similar elongated structure, but one was determined to be a disease pathogen, while the nonasbestiform fibers were less durable and damaging. Further complicating it was the presence of cleavage fragments, nonasbestos type fragments that might have a similar profile. Robert questioned which fibers were which in the counts of asbestos fibers in the mineralogist's final findings.

"Focusing just on the image, is the image itself and nothing else sufficient to determine to a reasonable degree of scientific certainty that this is asbestos or a cleavage fragment?"

The mineralogist couldn't contain his sarcasm. "If I close my eyes, I couldn't tell you that I'm sitting at a table. I can't think of a mineral that would give us that same chemistry and image other than asbestos. Also without a population of fibers, one hundred or more, which are not found, one has to assume based on many publications that if the fiber has the morphologic, EDS, and SAED criteria and is greater than five micrometers in length with an aspect ratio, length to width, greater than eight to one, it is an asbestos fiber and not a cleavage fragment."

Some of the jury members were beginning to get an inkling of the basic dilemma in front of them. It would become even more pronounced in the coming days. Both sides presented what they believed to be conclusive and credible data to bolster their arguments. Both sides maintained that they used the right tool for the right job. But just as someone can get the desired outcome of opening a tin can by using a screwdriver, it is not the best way, nor is it the choice a reasonable person would make. But one side in this courtroom knew what it was doing by deliberately using the screwdriver.

Chapter 27

Every morning since the trial began, Jane awoke with the intention of going to the courtroom. By the time she slowly made her arduous way from the bed to the bathroom, she understood that it was yet again not to be. She had no energy—not surprising since she had to force herself to eat the few morsels she could get down. The pain medication suppressed her appetite, but at least it numbed the brutal, stabbing jolts that wracked her with increasing frequency. With her weight loss, the waistband around her sweatpants had bunched into uncomfortable, tiny folds as she tightened the drawstring more and more to keep her pants from falling down.

It would have been easy to just stay in bed, but that meant giving in and giving up. No, she would do what it took and take whatever time she needed to make it to the bathroom and then to the breakfast table. She gripped her hands firmly on her new walker, rose up from the edge of the mattress, and placed one foot in front of the other with deliberate determination.

Jane's condition was also a growing concern in the courtroom. From Emily's report, the likelihood of her feeling well enough to testify was diminishing with each passing day. So, the decision was made to scrap it and screen the taped deposition. At least the jury had the benefit of seeing Jane in person in the gallery during those first few days. Human beings had become so adept at tuning out unpleasant emotions while watching tragedy and calamity on a television screen. From those two days watching her in the courtroom, they had a connection with her that mitigated any such passivity and detachment. The video would be played in full the next day once the judge had ruled on any and all objections the attorneys had originally lodged during the taping.

Moving up the supply chain, Emily's next witness was there to confirm that the same asbestos found in the raw talc was also present in the products that Jane had used daily over the course of decades. At least in the beginning, the learning curve was not as steep for the jury, since the technologies and methodologies to detect asbestos fibers, specifically electron microscopy, were similar to those outlined by the prior witness.

The pathologist on the stand was reporting on findings that built on a broader history of testifying at five or six other trials against the company and his cumulative testing of their various products that contained talcum powder. The written report had been submitted prior to trial as part of the discovery process and entered as an exhibit. It described how the products were purchased at retail and outlined the various different steps used to confirm the presence of a statistically significant quantity of the fibers.

While the defense would present its own contradictory findings when their turn came a few days later, Robert concentrated on trying to set the foundation for doubt about whether the pathologist's findings were reliable and credible. The objective was to try to poke holes at any appearance of ambiguity, from the theoretical down into the weeds. It was hard to dislodge from the ivory tower anyone with such lofty degrees and titles, prestigious academic positions, and a long list of authored scientific papers. So, one technique Robert used was to try to find other lofty-sounding scientists who might have differing opinions as to best practices and methods so as to muddy the arguments. If there happened to be a letter to the editor finding fault with one of those relevant, peer-reviewed studies the witness had coauthored, Robert did not let the opportunity slide to call that out, regardless of its relevance to the case.

On the testing protocols themselves, Robert grilled the witness on margins for error. Not every lab followed the same exact procedures, which might account for competing labs producing different findings. Emily was lying in wait and ready to pounce on this topic but knew to bide her time for a more strategic moment to confront the company's account.

Beating any already dead horse, Robert called attention to any appearance of bias and manipulation of the data to satisfy the client. The pathologist had the perfect riposte in describing how he had done work for both sides. "Sometimes a lawyer has told me point-blank not to bother writing up my findings when my data didn't support their case."

Diving in deeper, there was the reprise of the discussion of whether the count of fibers identified in his microscopes was really asbestos and not inflated by nonasbestiform or cleavage fragments. More debate followed about what were considered to be scientifically valid testing methods, Robert bringing up one particular protocol by name, accusing the pathologist of arbitrarily going beyond the search guidelines when he couldn't find enough conclusive data to validate his client's claims. "That standard you named is solely for detection of asbestos in air or water and has to be modified for a bulk sample analysis," the pathologist quickly countered to set the record straight.

The pathologist continued, "The problem with testing materials where the asbestos is a contaminate rather than an added component leads to a variety of issues." He described a number of variables that could not be accurately evaluated by a mineralogist's criteria. It was only through using the same criteria and definitions that are used for analysis of human tissue that it would be possible to definitively ascertain whether asbestos was present or not in the contaminate and at what quantity. "This analysis also helps us better define asbestos fibers versus a cleavage fragment from a similar nonasbestiform type."

That definition, the pathologist reiterated to make it absolutely clear, described the fiber as having the following attributes: parallel sides with a ratio of at least 3:1 to 5:1 length to width, five micrometers in length or greater, and with the elemental components and crystalline structure of an asbestos fiber.

Robert came back with another attack on the pathologist's protocol for identifying whether the crystalline structure of the fiber was that of an asbestos fiber or something else. "Do you use zone axis analysis in the SAED technique that requires the fiber to be tilted and rotated during analysis?"

The pathologist responded, "That technique is old criteria, extremely time-consuming, and has been documented in a number of recent publications by well-known and respected mineralogists that it is unnecessary with the newer transmission electron microscopes. Therefore, it is not done."

Being more thorough meant often erring on the side of caution because asbestos was not present in talcum powder in any uniform or standardized way in an individual container. Under questioning, the pathologist admitted that he had sometimes not found any asbestos in one sampling, while the next one might register substantial quantities. "Regardless, my experience has shown that if the sensitivity was increased by looking at more of the sample, asbestos would likely be found in each and every container."

What would be harder for the company to later defend was an adherence to testing methods that had a far lower bar of precision and sensitivity. It would seem ludicrous that a pathologist using the most sophisticated technology would be critiqued on one component of the methodology when the company's own experts had relied on only light microscopic techniques that were virtually incapable of seeing the fibers.

Chapter 28

The default most human beings use when confronting an unacceptable or unwelcome reality is to apply a strategy called denial. In most cases, it arises when we invent a fog of illusion to obscure what we fear the consequences might be. It is like refusing to go to the doctor when we know something is wrong. Our thinking is *If they don't find it, then I don't have it*. We can fool ourselves and others for a short while. When we are in denial, we serve our short-term benefit to the detriment of the highly preventable and more destructive outcomes to follow.

By this point, it was obvious to anyone on the jury with decent critical-thinking skills that Robert and the company he represented were also playing a denial game called plausible deniability. What he hoped was for the situation to degenerate into a kind of scientific "he said–she said" that would make achieving the required burden of proof unattainable for the plaintiff. It all depended on if Robert's experts who would testify later would project counterweight and then some.

Perhaps the greatest test was the testimony of Paul, the pathologist hired by Emily who specialized in the fiber burden analysis in human tissues. He had examined the paraffin blocks preserving specimens from Jane's two cancer operations. It was one matter to dispute the findings of whether there was asbestos in the mine or in the container of talcum powder. But it was all a preliminary to the ultimate smoking gun, whether Paul had found the type and quantity of fibers that demonstrably could have caused Jane's mesothelioma—and most importantly, if the exact type of fibers correlated to what was identified in the containers.

What followed during Emily's questioning went along with the same a thorough, step-by-step description of everything that happened from the moment Paul's lab received the tissue blocks to when he sent off his report with his findings. After first answering a series of questions designed to qualify him as an expert, Paul described in exacting detail how he prepared the specimens. He spoke of the rigorous tracking of each specimen so that it could be traced through every step back to its source. He described how the specimens were brought back to a state resembling living tissue and how solvents were used to dissolve the biological matter, leaving behind only the minerals or metals for analysis.

Emily had a good sense when the practices described stretched beyond a leap of faith—and the idea that Paul minced up a tissue sample in a blender and put caustic acid into it sounded like mad scientist stuff. A jury that took it all in with credulousness could just as easily be dissuaded by Robert's counterattack during cross-examination. So, she made a special point to dwell a little longer when she felt that a more rudimentary background explanation was needed.

Adding to the esoterica was how the reading of that remaining mineral soup (placed on a grid and put through energy dispersive spectroscopy and SAED analysis) could yield a reliable and realistic accounting identifying the specific type of fibers and their quantity.

Paul explained it like this: "The methodology I use for identifying and quantifying asbestos fibers in human tissue, whether in my clinical practice or in my consulting work, has been the same for over thirty years. My calculations are standard determinations in electron microscopy analysis, a relatively straightforward mathematical calculation of the total fibers per gram of tissue based on the quantity of material present, magnification, area analyzed, and the number of fibers found." He went on to say how the defense experts use the same exact procedure in their work that is consistent with the peer-reviewed literature. "They agree with me that finding one fiber in a tissue sample that is homogenized allows for extrapolation to the sample based on the limit of detection."

Emily asked, "Is that the same thinking that the police might use to estimate a crowd size in a large public space by counting up one grid and extrapolating it over the broader area of similar density?"

"Yes, it can be thought of in that way," answered Paul.

Paul went on to elaborate on what happens when asbestos fibers enter our bodies and how they end up in the tissues he studied. "Foreign materials, such as talc and asbestos, when inhaled, can deposit into the lung, pleura, omentum, and regional lymph nodes through the drainage of the lymphatic system." He explained how it is attacked in the lungs by white blood cells, monocytes, which mature to cells called macrophages, or resident macrophages, normally present in the lung, then migrate after taking up particles. Entering the lymphatic system, the fibers are then carried through that drainage and deposited into those tissues. In addressing how Jane's use of talc as feminine hygiene product resulted in her ovarian cancer, Paul explained that the exact mechanism of how it is transported is not totally understood, but it has been shown that the talc particles and asbestos can work their way through the female organs, the vagina, uterus, and fallopian tubes, to the ovary and abdominal cavity.

"The asbestos I identified in Jane's tissues, both ovarian and pleural, is truly countable asbestos and not cleavage fragments. In fact, some of the particles I found were bundles, meaning they can only be considered to be asbestos and not cleavage fragments." He concluded that the tissues in fact contained tremolite and anthophyllite asbestos, as confirmed by their chemistry (using the EDS technology) and by their crystal structure, as seen in the SAED patterns. He emphasized that his findings matched those of the pathologist who studied the containers of the talcum powder Jane used.

Cutting to the chase, Paul went to the heart of what the whole case rested on: "Jane had a substantial amount of platy and fibrous talc particles in large quantities in both her lungs and lymph nodes. Also found were typical contaminates of talc, aluminum silicates, and silica crystals. We identified substantial quantities of asbestos, both tremolite and anthophyllite types. When Jane's abdominal tissues, including her ovaries, fallopian tubes, uterus, abdominal pleura, and mesentery, were examined, similar to the lung and lymph node, asbestos fibers and particle distribution was found to be the same. The asbestos concentrations were found to be in the four thousand fibers per gram wet weight of lung or abdominal/ovarian tissue. The lymph tended to have more of the asbestos and the talc and the other contaminates because the lymph nodes are where the macrophages migrate to with all the particles and fibers they picked up in the lung."

"Do these findings correlate with other cases you have analyzed from patients exposed to cosmetic talcum powder?"

"They are very similar in types of particles and asbestos types seen and in similar amounts."

When it was his turn, Robert's strategy of attack during cross-examination mirrored much of the same as the last witness. He tried first to punch holes in the findings by attacking Paul's techniques. Paul answered calmly, "The opinions I offer in this case are rendered to a reasonable degree of scientific certainty, based on facts and data following generally accepted methods in the scientific community and backed up by peer-reviewed literature and consensus publications." He added again for emphasis how Robert's own experts also used the same methodology. Predictably, he asked if Paul ever testified for the defense. "I am available to test tissue and even containers of talc for whoever wants it. The problem lies in what I usually find. The defense doesn't like what I would testify to in depositions and in court, and I refuse to fabricate or lie. So, the defense does not use me."

All that Robert had left was to emphasize the ambiguity of where the asbestos came from.

He asked Paul, "Could not the asbestos fibers come from other sources? Is there any way to determine how the fibers or particles could have entered the body and from what product? How can anyone assume that all these particles and fibers could have come from an exposure that you cannot and have not identified from the multitude of products that are known to contain asbestos?"

Paul agreed that his findings could not shed any light on that. "Exposure histories are very important to attribute the fibers and the particles to the most reasonable source. Furthermore, a potential few days of say, a construction job in Jane's house, cannot compare to someone's breathing or absorbing these particles from daily or multiple-time-per-day exposures over years.

"Correlation of these human tissue findings with what is found and documented in the talcum powder containers and from the mines the talc was mined is the most supportive evidence of the human tissue source of the particles and fibers found."

The next day, the jury would get a fuller picture of this environmental exposure, both from Jane's taped deposition and from the testimony of an occupational medicine physician.

Chapter 29

The viewing of Jane's taped deposition could not have been timed better in Emily's mind. First of all, the jury had to sit through intense days of dense scientific presentations and debate. They certainly welcomed the opportunity to consider less taxing material. But there was method to the madness; the science gave them a better grounding to really appreciate the human impact part of the story now being presented.

It was a fair assumption that none of the jury members had ever been initiated into the intricacies of minerology and chemistry on the scale of particles magnified so many thousands of times. They could obviously all relate to ingesting things they could see and hold in their hands. About as far as they could comprehend about that nano-world were the germs that gave them infections and the molds and fungi that produced things like beer, wine, and cheese. Just as Jane was about to describe for them, they, too, had no way of considering the unseen, unfelt (and largely unpublicized) consequences of using a highly popular, ubiquitous product like talcum powder. But it also gave them pause to think about the whole universe of interactions between a complex living organism like the human body and a host of toxic foreign substances we encounter with every breath we take. Their deliberations that would begin in the very near future were sure to be a lot more complicated then they probably ever imagined.

Even though they were advised to keep an open mind, many of the jury members probably couldn't help starting their own silent, internal deliberations: If talc was really so dangerous, wouldn't there be many more millions afflicted like Jane? And wouldn't this be common knowledge, all over the news? Was the company being unfairly singled out when there could have been other undetected factors responsible for Jane's condition? After all, we're all going to die of something (and usually the interaction of several contributing factors). Perhaps her body's defenses and, more specifically, her immune system were undermined by genetics that predisposed her to any number of cancers, take your pick. Or was this more of a function of increasingly advanced modern technology that had newfound detection capabilities? It was legitimate to consider the economic incentives behind this and how this area of litigation had turned into one big cash cow.

The Jane they saw on the video screen taped several weeks prior was a clearly healthier-looking version than the one they had seen days ago in the courtroom. It was a stark reminder that all of the scientists' data they had just heard was dealing with still a living human being, not an impersonally dissected and analyzed collection of tissues. As much as she had tried to keep a strong continence on the video, discernable cracks in her appearance and demeanor revealed the truer extent of her damage.

The video allowed Jane to tell her own story in her own words, not the biased third-party interpretations of attorneys with vested interests. The viewers saw someone who projected sincerity, with an attitude of someone with little time left to waste and no appetite for nonsense. Beyond filling in all the blanks in her biography, Jane effectively short-circuited any speculation that there could have been other significant sources of exposure to asbestos that should be scrutinized in the proceedings. The fact that the defense did not mount any effort to discredit Jane or contradict any of her accounts was also blatantly obvious in its absence.

A medical doctor who was also an accredited industrial hygienist and specialist in occupational medicine was next to testify, there to help explain the nature of Jane's exposure to asbestos. After hearing about the insidious way that talc and the asbestos in it can pollute an environment, especially in a confining one like a bathroom, nobody in their right mind would willingly ever want to open a container of it again. She explained that when the powder is put in one's hand and then patted on the body directly or with a powder applicator, a significant amount of that powder gets into the air. The longer one remains in the confined bathroom, the more of the talc and its contaminants are breathed and enter the lungs. In addition, she stated that the longer the individual is in that bathroom, the greater amount of asbestos he/she will inhale because the asbestos fibers stay suspended in the air longer than the talc particles. The expert told how even the simple act of cleaning the bathroom counter or vacuuming the floor propelled the particles in the air, giving birth to a second new opportunity to enter our airways. She also confirmed what the experts before her had claimed, how the exposure to cosmetic talcum powder was the probable cause of Jane's two cancers, far outweighing any and all other smaller, isolated sources.

Emily than asked her, "What does it mean that Paul was able to find the talc and the tremolite and anthophyllite asbestos in Jane's tissues and not commercial type asbestos, namely amosite and crocidolite?"

She responded, "It is very significant, knowing that Jane had a substantial exposure to the cosmetic talcum powder. Add to that, it only has tremolite or anthophyllite type asbestos from the mines and in the talcum powder containers, based on previously published reports and results and containers studied for this trial. There was also no evidence of any other substantial exposure history. Given all of this, the only conclusion one can come to is that the asbestos that Jane used could have only come from the cosmetic talc that she was exposed to, and that was the causative factor in the initial development of Jane's ovarian cancer and later, as further proof, the development of her pleural mesothelioma—which is always attributable if asbestos can be identified in the tissue or in the exposures."

Robert waited for his chance to question this specialist in occupational medicine to launch into what he felt was his most vigorous proof of the plaintiff's uncertain claims against his client. Holding the paperwork in his hands, he asked the expert if she was familiar with a published study about the miners and millers in Italy who worked for a talc supplier to the company. "I am," she responded confidently.

"What we do know about the talcum powder we put into our products from the Italian mines is that three thousand workers were studied for seventy years, and not one of those workers got mesothelioma. If that mine was contaminated with asbestos sufficient to cause Jane's disease, then one of those workers would have shown some sign, after hundreds of times more exposure than you can possibly get from a container of our product. They showed no mesothelioma over a seventy-plus-year period. They showed no impact on lung cancer. That's the epidemiology that relates to the product, and none of those people got mesothelioma. How would you explain this documented finding of zero cases of mesothelioma among these workers?"

"You have to remember that mesothelioma can customarily take thirty, forty, or fifty years to sicken a patient. The sad reality is that most of these workers did not live long enough to develop mesothelioma. They were all men, many of whom were heavy smokers and a good number with coronary heart disease. Some developed pulmonary talcosis and silicosis from inhaling the dust. So, they usually died from other diseases that had faster onsets than mesothelioma. It also more than likely that many of these men also developed lung tumors for which the asbestos was synergistic with the smoking, causing the tumors sooner than each carcinogen would on its own."

The last expert Emily called before resting her case was someone trained to determine the value of monetary damages to be awarded if the jury came back with a guilty verdict. The calculations took into account much of the same actuary data insurance companies use to predict an average life span for someone with Jane's background and lifestyle. It also included a projection of lost earnings due to incapacitation and premature death. It also translated into dollars and cents the loss of family relationships and years of life cut short. Some economists, he shared, have set the value of an individual human year at about $130,000. Contrasting to that is the $160 estimate of the retail value of all the physical materials making up the human body.

The defense did its best to downplay the earning power of someone in her sixties like Jane. Robert tried his best to not sound crass in casting doubt that it was possible to put a dollar value on family relationships and the like. Emily would have preferred to rest her case on a less uncomfortable if not distasteful exercise. But that was the order and structure that cases like these generally followed.

Chapter 30

"If you drank a cup of coffee this morning, you had benzene because roasted coffee contains benzene and at least thirty other recognized carcinogens by the EPA. When you go into a coffee shop in California, there's a big sign on the door that says that this establishment contains products known to cause cancer. But nobody is concerned about drinking a cup of coffee. It's not going to do you a bit of harm unless you drink a large quantity of it. You may get the jitters but not cancer."

So began the case for the defense with a lecture on cancer (and how we get it) by an epidemiologist. First impressions do truly matter, and Robert wasted no time in trying to hammer home what he felt was the most reasonable argument for his client's innocence. The epidemiologist's coffee analogy was particularly poignant, he felt, because it underscored how we are bombarded with toxins with every breath, swallow, and step we take. Such thinking would lead someone to question how and why talc, as a single source among thousands of other potentially toxic molecules we encounter, should get all the blame. Although the slate of witnesses would do their best to support the product safety claims the company had made for generations, so what if talc had some trace amounts of asbestos, given our already blatant overexposure to cancer-causing compounds.

The epidemiologist went on to speak about another source of cancer, the radiation we encounter in dental x-rays, skiing at high altitude, or traveling in airplanes. "There is radiation in this courtroom as I speak. The EPA considers radiation to not have a threshold, meaning that any level can increase the chance of cancer, but we rarely pause to consider this a danger that might stop us from any of these activities."

The table was then set for the expert to completely downplay the importance of environmental factors, such as exposure to asbestos, to the cause of cancer compared to the consequence of underlying biological processes in the body. The overriding risk factors for mesothelioma, he maintained, were advancing age and the inheritance of a very rare gene mutation called BAP1. His research pointed to an extrinsic risk factor from exposure to asbestos but only from a very high level of amphibole fibers that are used in cement and other industrial applications and definitively not found in the company's cosmetic products.

The big buzzword in the testimony was "spontaneous," meaning that the cancers arise from a multitude of biological factors that he covered in detail, explaining the complexities of human cell biology. Our health, he explained, was dependent on the functioning of trillions of cells. To replenish our bodies, our cells are constantly dividing, with literally thousands of cell divisions going on at any given moment. "The complexity of that task when a cell divides into two daughter cells is like duplicating a book of a thousand pages with a thousand words on each page—without a single error. Most of the errors that occur in our bodies are innocuous. But as we age, the weight of these mutations becomes more serious, especially concerning those that regulate cell growth, which often trigger malignant cancers."

The epidemiologist gave the example of colon polyps that are discovered and removed during a colonoscopy. The polyps are premalignant lesions that result from mutation. Little by little, growth control is lost. If they eventually develop one or more critical mutations, they become cancerous.

Robert cut to the chase, asking if Jane's mesothelioma and her ovarian cancer occurred spontaneously. "Mesotheliomas, like other cancers, can and do occur spontaneously," the expert answered. "The majority of mesotheliomas among women in the United States today, whether pleural or peritoneal, especially peritoneal ones, do not have an asbestos etiology."

It sounded very familiar to Jane's first surgeon and his original explanation of her ovarian cancer as idiopathic.

Before ending his questioning, Robert put his witness on the record that in his expert opinion (and based on his review of Jane's records and the literature), her case would fall into the spontaneous category and not blamed on asbestos exposure. Moreover, he stated that there were no epidemiological studies implicating cosmetic talc increasing the risk for mesothelioma. The study concerning the Italian miners was brought up again in support of this claim.

Within seconds of beginning her cross-examination, Emily pounced on what she felt was the quickest pathway to discredit the epidemiologist. She asked him, "How many times did the term 'spontaneous mesothelioma' appear in your review of Jane's medical records?"

"It did not."

"Your opinion is that despite all of Jane's testimony about exposure to asbestos products, that her mesothelioma is spontaneous, right?"

"Yes, that is my opinion, and her strongest intrinsic risk factor was her age. In reviewing the entire epidemiological literature, even if all the allegations about exposure to talc and chrysotile asbestos are correct, her mesothelioma was not caused by exposure to asbestos."

"Is there a test that can be done to determine if someone's mesothelioma is spontaneous?"

"No, one has to rely on the epidemiology and the science of statistics and probability."

"In your assessment of Jane's case, if the talc contained chrysotile, tremolite, and anthophyllite asbestos, would you consider her two-decade-long, daily use of talc a significant exposure?"

"I do not know the level of contamination, and these calculations have to be done by an industrial hygienist."

Emily progressively tried to paint the witness into a corner. Going through a list of peer-reviewed research papers that had firmly established the scientific basis of asbestos as the sole cause of mesothelioma, the epidemiologist reverted back to his earlier testimony citing myriad other factors. On more pointed questioning, he denied that he had read the articles or, if he had, discounted their findings. The Italian miners made another encore appearance in one rebuttal. On similarly credible research identifying asbestos contamination in talc, his strategy was to discredit the qualifications of the scientists rather than the actual data itself. Questions about whether he had been privy to any testing results from either internal company reports or independent laboratories were deflected by stating that the lawyers did not give him access to such information.

Like a boxer seeing her opponent hanging on the ropes, Emily concluded with a laundry list of participation by this expert in other cases, where he had repeated the very same line of defense at each—and exclusively for the defense. As the epidemiologist was excused and walked past the jury to the exit, Emily felt she had accomplished what she set out to do. She wanted the jury to be left with the unsavory taste that this was a hired gun whose sole purpose was to please his clients and generate high revenues for his for-profit company.

Chapter 31

The journey to the airport and the ordeal of getting to the gate for his flight filled Neal with dread and contempt. In his younger years, any travel, whether it was for work or for pleasure, was a welcome diversion in his life. Being on the road made him feel more alive, connected with an almost childlike delight at the potential for new discoveries, adventures, and conquests. The change of routine was always welcome and invigorating, and all the new impressions from travel gave him a residual burst of inspiration.

Waiting by the gate, Neal perseverated on all the comforts of home he would forego over the next day and a half. Once on the plane, with the cabin doors shut, he easily retreated into his usual habits to make the time pass as quickly and as pleasantly as possible. Packed in his briefcase were options: a historical novel that he didn't make the time to read at home; his computer with a backlog of reports to review; and the file of prep material for his testimony the next day. With the aid of a cocktail or two, dozing off was also inevitable.

In the back of his mind was always the thought, *Maybe this is the last time I'll have to do this.* He took it almost as a slap to the face at this stage of his career that he was called on to do this. Just as he had been given the job to work in this division of the company years before, this also felt like a demotion, like he was being marginalized, sent off to do this kind of busywork when younger up-and-coming execs were given far sexier assignments.

He was arm-twisted just how mission critical this was for the company. These lawsuits were evolving into a major liability with the potential for a ballooning financial toll. There had been a few recent cases that had gone in the company's favor, but a high-profile victory here would send welcome reverberations. "You're our secret weapon," the higher-ups told him. "There is no one with the firsthand breadth of knowledge, the company history, and credibility than you. We need you on this one. There is much riding on it."

Neal reviewed the prep materials just to be on the safe side. Over the course of the last two years, he had represented the company more than a dozen times. There was no major deviation in the major bullet points. Rather, there were certain attributes that needed to be personalized for the particulars of Jane's case, life story, and medical history. Just as it was during the deposition, it was important for Neal to show respect for Jane and the misfortune that had befallen her. Being fluent with her personal details would help maintain that representation on the stand.

Grabbing his carry-on bag from the overhead, Neal disembarked and made his way through the congested corridors of LAX to meet his driver at baggage claim. The chauffeur adroitly took some backstreets and shortcuts to avoid the worst of the afternoon rush hour traffic. Within an hour, Neal checked into his hotel and, as habit dictated, surveyed the selection in the minibar. *Best to go easy*, he thought. He was due in court first thing in the morning and needed to be fresh.

While Neal was on the plane, Jane was on a journey of a different sort. Over the last several days, it had grown exceedingly hard for her to stay awake for any extended period of time. The heavy painkillers she was on sedated her into a place somewhere in between deep sleep and a drowsy nap. It wasn't to say that she wasn't completely unaware of people in her presence and what they were saying. But in some respects, she was like a film director creating her own scenes, blending her inner reality of subconscious dream fragments with the perceived outer world beyond the edge of her mattress. It wasn't all together so unpleasant. If an image came into her mind that was undesirable, she could with gentle ease ask it to depart and replace it with something much more acceptable. In that state, her dead parents came to visit her with a presence so realistic and convincing that it made her think their actual passing decades ago was the true illusion.

The situation staring Phil in the face was the one that no spouse wanted to confront. Jane's pain was excruciating, yet the palliative meds she was taking were bringing on a kind of dying stage on their own. To his delight and relief, she could snap out of the stupor quite spontaneously and stay in that state for an hour, perhaps two. She even found humor in her situation, coming up with a wisecrack that only she could. "Don't give me any vegetables, because I'm turning into one already!" It reminded him that the essence of the Jane he knew and loved was still present and accounted for.

As crass as it might sound, Phil flashed back to a far less complex quandary they faced when it was nearing time to euthanize their dog. The pet was clearly suffering and rapidly nearing his end. "He's not ready to leave us," Jane told Phil, trying to intuit the dog's psyche and the tail wagging that seemed to fly in the face of the considerable pain he was surely feeling. It was devastating making that judgment call between the selfish act of extending that life so precious to them versus doing the right thing to put the dog out of its misery.

Phil had a card in his desk for the hospice agency. The referral had already been made by the doctor. It was only a question of time, a hair trigger away, when to pick up his phone and activate it. "Not now, not yet," he said to himself, hoping that his sounder judgment was speaking now and not some delusional wishful thinking to remove the onus of that horribly consequential decision from his shoulders.

Throughout their ordeal, Jane and Phil would periodically visit the topic of last wishes. They had gone through the legal process of crafting living wills and durable powers of attorney. Moreover, Jane did not want to burden Phil or their children with any of the practical decisions. She made sure that all the funeral arrangements had been completed, down to the selection of a no-frills coffin so there would be no guesswork to her final wishes. She had checked the box "do not resuscitate," making it clear from the outset that she did not want any extraordinary measures of life support in her final stages. But all the best planning could not have prepared Phil for the real situation.

While Neal sat in his first-class recliner and Jane's consciousness cycled between dream and wakefulness, the work in the courtroom went forward. The day was consumed by the testimony of a geologist/mineralogist testifying on behalf of the defense. If there was a moment during the whole trial when jury members wished they could have had the day off, this was it. Boredom, confusion, frustration, overwhelm, and revulsion were just a few of the emotions they were all experiencing to greater or lesser degrees.

The new witness was a mineralogist hired by the company to testify. His task was simple—to discredit the findings of plaintiff's expert and demonstrate conclusively that the product was not contaminated with asbestos. Despite the fact that this expert's résumé was considerably thinner than Emily's pathologist who had identified the fibers in the talc samples, he went on full attack mode. "He did not follow the protocol that is accepted in all the literature … He failed to identify the minerals properly … His results are flawed and not reliable … He was confused and identified clearly nonasbestiform fibers as asbestos …"

As he showed slides and gave illustrations in support of his opinion, he just as well could have been speaking an indecipherable foreign language. Technical terms like "zone access diffraction analysis," acronyms such as R-93 testing methods, and complex coding for exhibits and samples like FA-113Q were flying back faster than the jury could compute. For good measure, the expert also maintained his adversary's shoddy laboratory procedures also contaminated the talc sample by a factor of potentially thousands of fibers. Anything on the photos of the grids he displayed that might have the appearance of being a smoking gun was summarily dismissed as a cleavage fragment. Before he was finished, he also took the time to discredit any earlier findings of asbestos in talc in the published literature. "They were using technology that is outdated, and they have since recanted their conclusions." When it came time to talk about the company's internal and commissioned testing of their talc dating back decades, the mineralogist argued conversely how similar protocols were still in use today as proof of their efficacy.

When Emily took over, she turned the tables to point out that the techniques the mineralogist used to analyze the talc for traces of asbestos were themselves outdated, primarily using inappropriate protocols that relied on data from light microscopy that were well under the necessary limit for accurate detection. They also squabbled over the definition of what a true asbestos fiber really looked like and how it could be distinguished from a cleavage fragment. Emily maintained that his evaluation focused on broader standards for geological evaluation at the exclusion of specific public health and safety determinants, which had been confirmed by governmental standards. Those official standards set forth the definition based on the shape of the fiber and its length-to-width ratio. Accordingly, Emily confirmed how it would be possible for the fiber and cleavage fragment analysis to have two different interpretations comparing the mineralogist's criteria versus the plaintiff's conclusions—again that were formulated from a public health perspective. She threw out the fact that the expert's commercial testing lab had been roundly criticized for this by the US Environmental Protection Agency in previous work. But the mineralogist stuck tightly to his script. It was his word against theirs, take it or leave it.

The jury needed to know a little more about the witness and his qualifications or lack thereof, Emily thought. She asked him to confirm that during his training, he had worked under a scientist who denied that asbestos was dangerous and believed that it did not cause disease. Her questioning established the fact that the expert had a fraction of the publications of her pathologist. Moreover, she called attention to his company's low reputation in the industry as being a shill to produce the findings his corporate clients wanted.

Winding up her cross-examination, Emily drilled down on what he knew about the biologic effects of these fibers. He claimed he did not know. "It is not in my area of expertise." He was equally evasive when asked if government standards required his mineralogic criteria. "I really don't know."

In closing, she asked him, "Do you believe that a cell can distinguish between a cleavage fragment or an asbestos fiber with the same measurements and overall structure? Is not the fact that these fibers caused a mesothelioma in Jane's pleura proof enough when asbestos is the primary cause of this disease and the pathologist you criticize had found the asbestos?" The expert just punted and stated again that he was not qualified to answer that question.

It felt like an act of mercy when the judge adjourned the court for the day.

Chapter 32

As the last day of testimony was about to begin, the world of the courtroom that had been so novel to the jury at the start had become oddly normal if not predictable. The rituals, the ground rules and etiquette, and the flow and rhythm had all assimilated into their consciousnesses like it had been an indelible part of their lives all along. Like an old married couple who completed each other's sentences, the jury became more adept at reading the participants, anticipating when an objection might be coming, when the judge might interrupt, how a counterattack might be executed, or even when a bathroom break would be called. The bailiff, court reporter, and clerk were no longer placeholders or cardboard cutouts but personalities to be studied, a welcome distraction when tedium struck. Undeniably, a sense of community had grown, a kind of trench mentality that made the artificiality and absurdity of the situation more bearable.

Outside in the corridor, Neal and Robert stood waiting for the bailiff to open the doors to start the day, just as they had done in other court buildings in other cities several times before. Neither felt the need for idle conversation or last-minute briefing. Neal was already brought up to speed on any specifics that might deviate from his script. Moments later, they walked in together, with Neal taking his seat in the gallery in the first row behind the defense table.

As the doors closed, the jury filed in, and the rest of the cast of players shuffled around and got settled. Before the judge entered, the doors opened once again. The bailiff suddenly got up and went over to help hold open one of the doors as a woman in a wheelchair entered. In that second, the unremarkable routine that usually typified the start of each day vanished.

Some of the observers may have viewed this as a welcome development to up the tension and spice up what had been a pretty dry affair to date. Others dreaded what might degenerate into an uncomfortable display of emotions that they could just as well do without.

The last thing that Jane wanted was for anyone to think that her surprise appearance in the courtroom that morning was for theatrics, to make a scene, to have some premeditated intention to have influence on anybody or anything. None of that mattered to her. If she could have taken a pill and become invisible at that moment, she would have taken it. She wanted no attention, no sympathy, no one fussing over her or otherwise bombarding her with their own discomfort at seeing her in her condition. For that reason, she was granted permission by her doctor to unplug her IV fluids for the day. The only tube she would have with her was for the portable oxygen she needed.

She had kept up with the proceedings, getting the broad strokes as Emily had promised to do. She knew that the company that produced the products that she had so trustingly and loyally used all those years was going to tell their side of the story that morning.

She knew that this day was coming a few days in advance. "Are you really certain you're up for this?" Phil had asked her early that morning. He quickly realized he was wasting his breath.

"I'm going. Period."

Understandably, Neal had a second or two delay in figuring out what was causing the big stir. When he realized that Jane was there, recognizing her from the picture in his file, he went into his default position of doing his utmost to ignore her presence. He had been through this situation a few times before in other trials where victims and/or their families made sure to be in attendance. Up to this point, his technique of filtering them out had worked efficiently. To use a sports analogy, it is how golfers making the last putt for a championship can tune out any and all distractions, either in their field of vision or their thoughts, concentrating solely on the line to the hole in front of them.

If someone had asked her while she waited there in the moments before the proceedings began why she wanted to be there, or what she hoped would happen, her explanation would have probably been unsatisfactory to the questioner. Her life to date (and all her misfortune) had taught her that having well-defined expectations of desired outcomes often led to harsh disappointment. Instead, in her innermost intentions, she was not much different from the jury members who sat there with her. It was all about discovery. She was there as a listener. In some ways, the stakes were about something more important to her than her case, on whether injury was done to her or what retribution might be owed her for it. In the strangest sense and much to her own astonishment, she had already moved beyond those considerations.

As she sat there, her mind danced in a different realm than the time and space around her. She pondered the substance of her life, everything that she had believed in her heart, everything that she strove to do in her work, the caring she tried to infuse in her relationships with her husband, her children and grandchildren, her students and colleagues, and with complete strangers she would probably never meet again. Did all of it or any of it really matter? Was that idealism she had carried since early childhood of being a force (albeit tiny) for a better world just a fool's game?

She didn't know whether anything she would see or hear that day would give her any answers. For now, she had the peace of mind to know that she had gotten herself together to be there. It was the right thing to do. She felt she owed it to herself.

Chapter 33

Trust is the precious bedrock of human relationships. It was Neal's assignment to defend that trust or at least do what he could to contain the threat. Most reasonable adults can be forgiving up to a certain point. Everyone makes mistakes. We recognize that often our mistakes can trigger innovation, the scientific method case in point. But intention is everything—and intention was still very much in question as Neal took the stand.

It was a fair assumption that many of the jurors had come far enough in their thinking to think there was fire where they smelled smoke. They knew by this time that lawsuits were propagating. They had also been initiated into an appreciation of all the science that went into this discussion. Through what they already knew and had come to learn, they may have given talc and asbestos a kind of benefit of the doubt, in the same category as lead and mercury, that had been in common use for centuries and considered safe until science became sophisticated enough to uncover their hidden harm. Neal made sure to hammer this home, talking about all the ancient uses of talc, including the Egyptian amulets.

Robert began his questioning by reading from an important company document. "We believe our first responsibility is to doctors, nurses, and patients, to mothers and fathers and all others who use our products and services." Robert asked if Neal was familiar with the statement.

"This is the company credo. Every employee has a laminated copy of it on their desks," Neal answered. "It is also framed in the lobby of the building, so everyone can read it when they go past every day."

"The document goes on to state, 'We're responsible to the communities in which we live and work and to the world community as well. We must be good citizens.' How has this influenced your work?"

Neal described how the company had regular meetings to discuss the credo and talk about how each person put it into action in their daily work.

Lastly, Robert read one more statement. "'Our final responsibility is to our stockholders. Business must make a sound profit. We must experiment with new ideas. Research must be carried on, innovative products developed, and mistakes paid for.' How did this factor into your work?"

Neal chalked it all up to the idea that if you got the first part right and you behaved properly and responsibly to the whole community, everything else would fall into place. The company would succeed and make a profit. Robert went on to describe the care that went into each of their products and the rigorous testing that conformed to industry standards and many times exceeded them.

"And that was the case on your talc products?"

"I believe so, yes. If you look at the amount of testing that's been done on our talcum powder over one hundred years, it's phenomenal, especially over the last forty years."

"Would you personally ever sell a product if there was a serious concern about the health and safety of a customer?"

"No, I wouldn't."

"In the almost forty years you have been with the company, would the company ever sell a product knowing that it could cause cancer?"

"No."

"Has the company ever been in the asbestos business? ... Has it ever mined or milled asbestos? ... Has it ever made products that contain asbestos? ... Is asbestos a mineral that the company has ever wanted in its products?"

Neal emphatically replied no to all these questions. "It has been known for over one hundred years that asbestos has hazardous effects."

Jane sat impassively as she listened, wishing again she could conjure a cloak of invisibility. Under no circumstances did she want to become a focus or distraction that might divert attention away from the witness. The jury did not need her editorial input. So, there were no eye rolls, no angry glares, no pursed lips, no gestures of any kind that might reveal her emotions or what she was thinking. But it also served as self-preservation. It was like she was on a power-save mode to ration whatever energy she had left. Her endurance during the two days she attended the beginning of the trial was poor and presumedly worse now in her current state. She wanted above all to make it to the end of the day and to hear all that was said.

That said, it didn't mean Jane's sense of indignation and disgust at what she was hearing was somehow pacified. It was of course a given that Neal would do all to portray the company as a victim, afflicted by its own form of metastasizing cancer with all this unwarranted litigation. Throughout its history and especially during these contentious times, the company had not wavered one iota from its claims of product purity. So, Jane was fully clear that today would not be any different. The only surprises awaiting discovery, she surmised, would be in the degree of audacity and the skillfulness in defending the indefensible.

Had she been feeling better, it may have been more difficult for her to stifle expressing what she was experiencing on the inside. The first instance was when Neal talked about the company credo, emphasizing how pleasing the shareholders would be a fait accompli if their products and services served the highest good of their consumers and the community. Jane was savvy enough to know that such a statement had rotted well beyond its expiration date. It may have been partially true generations ago when the document was first written. But the reality was that the scientists were no longer calling the shots. Most big corporations were run now by financial people who knew the inner workings of a bank far better than a factory or laboratory. There were more profits to be made by moving assets around than by actually making and selling their products. The cringeworthy cynicism of this was only amplified moments later when Neal outlined just how insignificant talc products were to the company's bottom line, a very small drop in the bucket of profitability. "It is a product that is an important part of our history and our branding. And it has a hundred-year history of safety." In Jane's mind, Neal was summarily dismissing her as equally trivial, worthless like the nickels and dimes that barely show up on a spreadsheet.

Over the next two hours, Robert and Neal worked systematically through the document load that was ultimately where the company's case rested, the majority of which was the same contained in the folder he had been presented with when he started overseeing the brand. It all painted a portrait of meticulousness, with no stone left unturned at every level of the process. They wanted the jury to be convinced that no other product on the face of the earth had gone through this level of testing, conducted by the most trusted research laboratories, using the best available technologies. For good measure, the Italian miners were dredged up again, as if no further convincing was needed.

The court was adjourned for lunch break with plans for Emily to begin her cross-examination when they resumed. Jane made her answer clear when Phil asked if she was game to continue. They decided to retreat to the quiet and privacy of their car, so Jane could recline and rest. A staffer in Emily's office was tasked with getting them some takeout from a nearby restaurant.

Chapter 34

As Neal took the stand after the lunch break, Emily looked over her notes one last time before beginning her cross-examination. A lot was riding on what would come out of the next few hours, but you wouldn't sense anything was out of the ordinary based on the demeanor of the sparring partners. Neal's confidence was grounded in doing what he felt had thus far been a skillful defense of the company. More importantly, he seemed to have an effortless and unwavering command over the details of all the talking points and supporting documents. There was no need for hesitation to refresh his memory or punt on any details. When Robert mentioned a certain test and the techniques used, Neal could almost recite by heart all the sundry details with a familiarity and fluency like he had been in the laboratory doing the work himself.

Neal was being the tortoise in the race against the hare, plodding slowly and steadily—cool and collected, calm and confident. There was no need for dramatics, emotion, or showy rhetoric. The company had been in existence for well over a century, and there was no reason to doubt that it would still be there one hundred years later. Perhaps lurking under it all was a condescending if not patronizing tone that believed there was no way the jury could truly appreciate or begin to digest the complexity of the content. In fact, Neal had hoped they would have already thrown their hands into the air long before hearing from him. Instead, he was betting on the notion that the panelists would be making their decision largely based on his sincerity and gentle but firm persuasion. The company also had so much goodwill banked through all of their products as a trusted friend of the family for generations. So, his playbook was simply to live and breathe and otherwise be the living embodiment of the credo Robert had brought up earlier in the day.

Emily's playbook borrowed from a different children's story idiom. It was a fable everyone knew. She was wagering it would sock a knockout punch, easily comprehensible and with a credible dose of common sense to the jury. Quite simply, Neal and the corporation he represented were foxes guarding the chicken coop, very well-tailored, manicured, and polished ones at that.

Perhaps the biggest blemish on capitalism and the American form of democracy in recent years was the hegemony of big business over the interests of the common people, with unmistakable consequences on the diminishing quality of life in America. Closer to home, the marriage between political interests and the economic interests of the corporations had become all too blatant in the relaxing of regulation and oversight. The relationship could grow downright incestuous with the revolving door of politicians becoming board directors, high-powered attorneys, and lobbyists for those special interests. Add to that list all of the former regulatory agency governmental policymakers who got hired away to lucrative positions in the industries they formerly oversaw. Worse yet was all the corporate underwriting of academic institutions, putting their fingers on the scale of what research got done and the degree to which their findings could be trusted. At the end of the day, the checkbook ruled. For the right amount of money, anything was possible, and anybody could be bought.

Emily did not want to turn this exercise into an economics, social policy, and ethics lesson. But at moments like this, she drew strength and inspiration by again thinking about the lethal injustices perpetrated against her Armenian forebearers. At least here in America, courts were still the last best chance to do the right thing, she thought. She gave full credit to the jury's intelligence level to put two and two together before she wrapped up the day's work. It also didn't hurt that Jane was there in the back row as a living victim of these policies and practices and the epitome of the underdog against a goliath of a company. She was exhibit A, and it was impossible to turn a blind eye to her.

The further along Emily got into her questioning, Neal's perfect plate glass veneer and easygoing countenance began to show crow's feet. His body language became more defensive, arms crossing until he noticed it and corrected his posture, tugging occasionally at his collar as if his necktie had become a tightening noose.

There was much to unpack. In almost every study, research finding, and laboratory testing that the defense had presented during Neal's testimony, there were holes everywhere, some huge and others seemingly nitpicky but significant all the same. Emily could have spent two days dissecting each matter, pointing out the errors, deceptions, and ambiguities. But that was not to be. The jury's patience was surely running thin, the sand running down to its last trickle. They had their eyes on the exit. Instead, Emily cherry-picked what she felt was the most egregious. Her strategy was to let them extrapolate and do the math, trusting it would lead to the burden of proof required.

Emily's strategy was to illustrate the common thread that the company was deliberate and premeditated in doing whatever was necessary to hide any findings of contamination of asbestos in talc and, more important, bury the fact that they knew anything about it. In fact, once the curtains were pulled back on the degree to which the deck of deception had been stacked, it would effectively call into doubt any evidence the company put forward.

Emily began by accusing the company of systematically exploiting the lower product safety testing accountability for cosmetics versus the far more rigorous, fine-tooth protocols the FDA demanded of pharmaceutical drugs. She pointed out the fact that the company was a founding member of the industry organization called the Cosmetics, Toiletries, and Fragrance Association (CTFA) that developed and policed those standards. Other watchdog organizations as far back as 1934 had already published reports about the hazards of asbestos. But the company did not heed any calls to examine their products until many decades later. Moreover, she pointed out how the company had a hundred-year history of selling talc products before they did any testing on it.

"Around 1971 was when there started to be some really bad publicity about asbestos in talc. Isn't that correct?" Emily asked. "Isn't that the real reason why the company started testing?"

"I don't know about the publicity piece," Neal countered. "I can tell you that there was a meeting with the FDA in August 1971 where they were looking into cosmetic-grade talc. At the same time, the trade organization started looking into it. By September of that year, the company was developing analytical methods so we could analyze the talc we were using."

Emily stated, "According to the company documents we have, didn't something change around 1974 with regard to talc processing—and why?"

Neal paused for a second or two before responding. He knew that he had to be careful here, entering into some vulnerability for perjury. He was not in a position to refute the documents Emily had that were not making the company look too good. So, he did his best to spin it in the most favorable light possible. "Results of testing prior to 1974 indicated that there was some asbestos identifiable even by the light microscopic techniques. It was at this point that the company modified its processing of the talc to eliminate the asbestos. They were able to eliminate some but not all the asbestos. But they deemed it at a level they could still characterize as 100 percent safe."

Neal went on to explain that they were using a two-step process utilizing x-ray diffraction to test whether the mineral was present, followed by optical microscopy to see if it existed as a fiber. A few years later, the company started with a third-party firm to "independently" confirm the negatives they were getting. Emily pointed to an internal company report and asked Neal how the company could defend these practices in light of the FDA expressing grave concerns about the accuracy of the methods absent comprehensive electron microscopic analysis.

Holding in her hand some additional internal documents, Emily quizzed Neal on efforts by the FDA at that juncture to step in and regulate talc. "They even proposed a regulation. Isn't that correct?"

"Yes."

"But your company, through the CTFA, more or less told them, 'We have this. Let us self-regulate first.' Correct?"

"I don't have the documents on that, but my understanding is that there was a discussion of the best test methods to measure asbestos."

"The question is, did the CTFA and your company tell the FDA, 'Instead of the government passing a regulation, let us self-regulate'? That's what they did, didn't they?"

"I'm not disagreeing with you, with the tone of what you're saying, but I don't know the exact words of how they characterized it."

"So, the FDA never ended up regulating asbestos in talc. Correct? The CTFA told the FDA that they'd work with them to develop methods, so they'd all be on the same page.

"According to this internal company document, let me ask you to verify this—'we believe it is critical for the CTFA to now recommend these methods to the FDA before the art advances to more sophisticated techniques with higher levels of sophistication.'"

"Yes, I know this was an issue at the time."

Neal referred back to the trade organization and its recommendations. "The methods adopted, the CTFA J4-1 method, is the one that's still used today. It's also used in the US Pharmacopeia, so it has a lot of history of valid use. It is very well regarded in the published literature. So I'm not sure where the shortcomings are coming from."

"Are you aware that J4-1 is a testing method for asbestiform amphibole minerals?'

"Yes."

"Chrysotile, for example, is not an amphibole mineral, is it?'

"Chrysotile is not."

So, as Emily questioned further, she told how the trade organization applied this testing protocol to do a comprehensive industry-wide test, including the company's product and other talc-based brands in 1974. And they came back with the good news that none of the products contained asbestos. If an outside laboratory reported some positive tests with minute quantities of asbestos, the FDA took the company's word that this was a random contamination.

Emily then asked, "Wasn't this only after you had modified your methods of preparing the talc because it had been identified not only by the industries-approved techniques but also by electron microscopic identification?"

Neal answered, "Yes, that is true."

Before leaving this topic, Emily read from one last report, which was the company's defense for using the J4-1 test and for not relying on some of the much more sensitive electron microscope methods talked about earlier in the case, like SAED and TEM. "It says here that they haven't been adopted since they suffer drawbacks, and it says the amount of material under examination is small, and the time for analysis, expertise required, and expensive equipment eliminate them as routine methods, right?

"Yes, that's what the report stated, yes."

"And did you view that as a fair criticism?"

"It's not unreasonable to recognize that not everyone has the expertise with transmission electron microscopy. Having said that, you can go outside and find experts who can help you."

Next, Emily honed in on another common method the company used to counter findings they didn't like; they would hire a scientist at an institution of equal stature to run their tests on the same sample. Predictably, the new results would be more to their liking. They covered their asses, saying, "In essence, within the limits of detectability, we cannot positively identify any asbestos-type minerals in the final product samples." If a lab happened to find it, they could sugarcoat it with the rationale that "just because asbestos is present in the material doesn't mean it's necessarily dangerous."

Remarkably but not surprisingly, one leading scientist who came back with a damning report retracted it shortly thereafter. He admitted, "I may have been mistaken. Some talcum contains a lot of asbestos, and others very little. The sample from the company happens to be very pure talc."

Emily showed more documents that showed that this practice was not a one-off.

"Do you see from time to time where people have to correct things and make adjustments?"

"Yes, yes."

"Is that common in the science area, particularly with this kind of technology?"

"It is. It's very often the case of let's check that result. That wasn't what we were expecting. Let's go back and check."

Emily read from the revised report. "'Here is our modified thinking. After looking at several fresh samples on the light microscope, we have not been able to substantiate the tremolite levels we originally reported.'"

"As you look at this back and forth, do you see anything that gives you pause as to anything improper going on?"

"No, like I said, it's not unusual with scientific studies that you—if you get an unexpected result, you want to check that out."

When both attorneys declared that they had no further questions, the judge told Neal that he was excused, and the proceedings were adjourned for the day. Neal looked up at the clock in the courtroom with a sense of relief that the ordeal was over and there was more than enough time to get to the airport for his flight back home. He nodded to Robert as he made his way past and paused briefly as he went past Emily. At that moment, his mind conjured up the metaphor that he had just gone sixteen rounds in a heavyweight boxing match. The referee stood between them, waiting for the judges to declare a winner, although it seemed too close to call. He looked at Emily with a subtle nod of respect given to a worthy adversary who had fought a good fight.

As he waited by the curbside for his driver to pick him up, Neal suddenly felt he was being watched. About twenty-five feet away to his immediate left was a parking space reserved for the disabled. He slowly turned and brought his eyes into focus on the eyes that were watching him. Jane was sitting in her wheelchair as Phil was opening the passenger side door to help her into the car.

Try as she might, Jane could not avert her frozen gaze. She had listened to this person trying to disavow any intention or behavior that would have any bearing on what had become of her. In these few seconds, with every ounce of energy that she had remaining and could muster, she demanded to be seen by him. There were no words she wanted to say. She had even given some thought to how such an encounter might sound that morning as she dressed. But nothing she could think of was good enough; nothing could condense and distill the magnitude of her disappointment and disillusionment.

If her glance for those few seconds could say anything to Neal, she hoped it would be this: "Understand the enormity of my heartbreak. I am powerless to think that I can change you; nor can I expect that you will change on your own accord. My eyes are peering into your soul, and I see the desolation that you are unable and are incapable of seeing for yourself. I bear no malice toward you. You are just a replaceable cog in a repugnant machine. There are millions of others who would gladly do your job. My heart breaks for you for your abandonment of your humanity. My eyes are asking you, was this all worth it?"

Chapter 35

The courtroom came to order in what all hoped would be the last day before the case went to the jury. Sensing the fatigue factor with diminishing attention spans, Judge Sanchez decided that she would give the jury their instructions as the first order of business. This was a more complicated case than most, in her opinion, given how much rested on the convoluted and often conflicting interpretations of science. She repeated again, lest they had forgotten, that the burden of proof was not "beyond a reasonable doubt," as in a criminal case, but rather a lower bar of "more likely than not."

Throughout the proceedings, it was natural that each of the jurors kept what amounted to an internal scorecard, a tally of moments when one side put forward a more convincing argument than the other. It was a lot more subjective than they would have liked. Final impressions were often colored as much by the actual substance as by how well acted it was in the delivery. They had learned early on that any resemblance to courtroom drama portrayed in film or television was sorely lacking. A good portion of the time they had sat with strained patience and varying degrees of feigned attention through often tedious and boring expository passages. Mercifully, cross-examinations were more exciting. Sparks would fly back and forth, and curiosity was triggered when trying to figure out who was bullshitting whom.

Judge Sanchez had been to this rodeo many times before. She knew what was sorely needed was a kind of cheat sheet they could each use to quickly cut through the mishmash of impressions and separate wheat from chaff. There would be verdict forms to guide their deliberation, but more detailed explanation was needed. The jury members sat up and listened with rapt concentration to the judge's words, knowing that it was for their benefit and would hopefully make their work more expeditious.

"To establish this claim, the plaintiff must prove all of the following four points. Firstly, that the company manufactured, distributed, or sold the product. Secondly, that the product contained a manufacturing defect when it left the company's possession. Thirdly, that Jane was harmed. And lastly, that the product's defect was a substantial factor in causing Jane's harm. If the answer is yes to all of these, then, did the plaintiffs prove that Jane personally used a container or containers of the product that contained a sufficient amount of asbestos to be a substantial factor in causing her disease?"

The judge went into further detail about how best to determine if the company had acted in a responsible or irresponsible way toward Jane and other consumers. The overarching issue was whether the benefits of the design of the product far outweighed the risk. In discerning that, she asked them to consider the gravity and likelihood of potential harm from using the product. Could the company have feasibly come up with a safer, affordable, and advantageous alternative design at the time of manufacture?

One last but hardly least consideration she put in front of them was whether the company willfully misled Jane, knowing the potential risks presented a substantial danger to her, and failed to adequately warn or instruct her of that risk. The bottom line they needed to determine was whether the company's negligence in providing sufficient instructions or warnings was a major factor in causing Jane's harm.

As Emily began her closing argument, she was giving a refresher course, condensing two weeks' worth of testimony into a little more than forty-five minutes. It gave the jury a kind of checklist to compare their internal scorecards with hers, seeing if they had forgotten or overlooked anything of importance. She gave them the gift of hindsight. It was understandable that they had grown in their depth of knowledge about the case the longer the trial went on. Emily provided them a chance to reassess, based on the fuller context of hearing the entire case presented.

"We're not going to redo the trial," Emily assured them. "But things came in in different orders and at different times, and the hope is that I can organize things in a way that allows you to see how it fits with the law that the court just read. And then you can apply the facts to the law, and you'll do that back in the jury deliberation room.

"I want to remind you who this case is about. I know that you got to see Jane here in court for just a few days but only heard her words on videotape. As you could see yesterday, she is very, very sick. You will be able to go home and enjoy time with your families, but Jane is hardly in a condition to do so any longer, and it is a really devastating situation to be in, especially if you take into account that this disease that is destroying her life, mesothelioma, could have been prevented and should have been prevented. Her life is being cut short by an estimated seventeen point two years because of this."

Giving a brief synopsis of Jane's medical history, through all the biopsies, surgeries, and treatments for ovarian and pleural cancers, Emily hammered home the amount of pain and suffering and horrors Jane had been through. "And now she wakes up every morning and wonders if it is going to be her last."

The thread that Emily wove through every point she brought up was how the company acted with negligence and malice at almost every step along the way. "Every single positive test that came back was an opportunity for the company to do the right thing. Every single time, they did the wrong thing. They continued to sell the product with no warnings, even though there was direct evidence for many years that the talc alone could cause injury, even without the asbestos-causing granulomatous lung disease. They continued to not warn, to not notify people like Jane of the potential that asbestos was in their product, giving her the opportunity to make a different decision. They hid the fact that they had known from their own testing that their product had significant amounts of asbestos, and in and around 1974, altered the way they processed this talc to remove the asbestos. However, their own documents show they knew that it was not possible to remove it all. Further, they then produced an alternative to the talcum powder using corn starch as an alternative but never gave any indication why. It is the definition of a willful and knowing disregard of the rights and safety of another."

Reminding the jury of how the company purposefully manipulated the data to get the results they wanted, she used the analogy of the proverbial deer in the headlights but with a different twist. Using their technology, the company was effectively using their low beam lights. Had they used their high beams, they would have seen the deer and prevented the accident.

"You've heard a lot of evidence from a lot of different experts, scientists, doctors, epidemiologists, geologists, and biologists. I think this case is really about common sense, and I want each of you to use your common sense as you sift through all the evidence." As a counterpoint, she asked them to consider how the defense had presented a lot of confusing evidence. "They tried to confuse what asbestos is versus a mineral, what asbestiform is versus nonasbestiform, what a cleavage fragment is versus an asbestos fiber. The important issue here is not what one calls the mineral but how the mineral can affect the cells to alter them in becoming a cancer cell. Although the defense's expert brought up this issue of asbestos and nonasbestos, Paul unquestionably demonstrated that there were asbestos fibers taken from Jane's tissues. Furthermore, the defense could in no way convince us that it came from another source other than the talcum powder products Jane used for all her life."

Emily concluded, "If you know that your product contains asbestos and you fail to inform your consumers of that, you fail to warn and you hide that information from someone like Jane, that is the definition of despicable."

After a short break, it was Robert's turn to give his closing statement. After Emily's blistering attack, Robert tried to deflate some of the tension in the room by taking a different tact, a charm offensive of sorts. He joked with them how the free candy the court gave them made them happier jurors and helped them get through the case. He went to some length to compliment them for their patience and perseverance, sounding more like a concert diva thanking his ticket holders for coming out and being such a wonderful audience.

"So, what you've heard has been plaintiff's relying on old science that has been debunked," charged Robert in his opening salvo. "It's been debunked since the 1970s, and now it's coming back again." He went on to substantiate this by saying how the most damning findings from Paul's work that identified asbestos in their talc products has never been reproduced by any other scientist. "The only person who said it is true is Emily, and the court has instructed you that anything the attorneys tell you is not evidence." He also added that Emily's expert witnesses had testified on plaintiff asbestos cases for a minimum of thirty years, so the jury should take that into consideration. To ensure it was heard the first time, Robert repeated how the company's experts were far more distinguished and better qualified than the plaintiffs', who used largely discredited methodologies and bogus math.

Robert's strategy was to state how unsubstantiated the attacks against the company were by recapping the conflicting findings about the raw talc from the source mines, the epidemiology and case studies, and, finally, the testing methods. There were no case reports or epidemiological studies showing that cosmetic talcum powder had caused asbestos disease, down to the miners and millers in the mines in Italy. If talcum powder from the mines was going to cause mesothelioma, you would see it in the millers and miners, their family members, factory workers, and so on down the line to the end consumers.

He further accused Emily of advancing a conspiracy theory that the company was somehow colluding with the CTFA to use test methods that were not sensitive enough to find asbestos. "Even one of the plaintiff's experts admitted that the company's testing protocols were state-of-the-art today, as they were in the 1970s. That expert also testified that the outside laboratory that the company used was a premiere facility, and how the company was being reasonable and responsible for the testing methods they used. Emily chose not to remind you of that in her closing statement."

Robert went through each of the mines that had provided the company with raw talc, refuting any claim that the product was contaminated with asbestos, listing all the international and national institutes from the WHO downward that never identified asbestos in testing results. "The testing methods the plaintiff's experts relied on have actually been debunked. That literature was shown just not true because the testing methods that they were using did not distinguish between asbestos and not asbestos. I know that the plaintiff doesn't like the term 'cleavage fragment.' But a cleavage fragment is not asbestos, and the noted epidemiologist who testified before you has concluded from an animal study that cleavage fragments do not cause disease."

Emily remembered the detailed discussion with Paul about cleavage fragments during the deposition. He had mentioned to her how Robert's point was true only in the context of particular ones that were in the form of chunks and not the fiber-like ones Paul had identified that could be cancer causing. She scribbled a note to herself to bring this up in her final remarks if time permitted. It was getting into the weeds, but she thought this was a good case in point on how the defense manipulated and shoehorned data incorrectly to support its claims. She also flagged Robert's claim that Paul's results had not been duplicated. "Bring up other authors of peer-reviewed paper who did their substantiating analyzes independently," she wrote on her notepad.

Robert spoke next about the levels of asbestos exposure in the environment that could be in background levels in buildings and perhaps the very school where Jane taught. "It could be a hundred thousand times more than Jane's purported exposure through talc, yet no one is talking about cellular changes from that."

Jane's disease was age, Robert reemphasized, again repeating the theory that ovarian cancers were naturally occurring, "spontaneous" diseases. "Jane's cancer has nothing to do with anything that happened at the company. It's very sad. It's been emotional, but when you look and unpack from the scientific side, there's just no evidence that the product had anything to do with her disease."

As customary, Emily had one last opportunity to rebut. "Can the company really claim that their mines were clean when their own testing data said they were not?" She leafed through the exhibits in the file in her hand and read aloud blurbs from page after page of test results positively identifying asbestos in all the mines from which the company bought raw talc. "As you can hear, chrysotile, tremolite, and anthophyllite asbestos were found in varying amounts in the vast majority of their tests.

"Defense's counsel has no other option than to falsely claim that the science was old and the scientists less experienced than his because there is no other way to contradict the hardcore, damning evidence, photographic evidence discovered by the pathologists. The samples Paul examined with the electron microscope from Jane's tissue revealed the presence of fibers that met all definitions of an asbestos fiber. These corresponded with the findings of asbestos in the product. The other side wants you to believe these are all cleavage fragments. All they were left to do is try to shoot the messenger, finding fault with protocols and technologies more sophisticated than theirs and degrading the work and reputations of scientists of high standing. In fact, their expert on this has distinctly less experience and only more narrowly focused on mineralogy."

Emily felt the clock running down on her, so she left the jury with one last thought. "You all are in a unique position as the conscience of the community. You get to decide what is reasonable for our community and what is not. And you get to speak directly to the company in this situation. You truly get to have the last word. This case will be up to you. Please use your common sense. I really, truly do thank you for your time."

With that, Judge Sanchez adjourned the case for the day, ordering the jury to begin their deliberations the next morning.

Chapter 36

For two days, the jury deliberations dragged on. At various times, they put in requests to review documents, which were the only tea leaves those outside the room could read to decipher any progress and possible sticking points. If there was any noticeable trend, it was that they wanted to more closely examine opposing reports side by side, whether from the mineralogists, the pathologists, or the laboratories. They also wanted to build their own timeline from the internal company documents, correspondence with the FDA, and any public-facing pronouncements from advertising and press releases to see if there were any obvious reactive patterns and overtly protective measures.

On the inside, there were some who had already made up their minds from the moment they first set foot into the deliberation room. Those few came under scrutiny from their fellow panelists, checking to make sure they were not acting too rashly or were somehow biased in one way or another to such a degree that they could not carefully analyze the evidence from both sides. There were others who were quite frankly stymied at the complexity and the harshly conflicting fact universes each side presented. For the latter, scrutinizing the requested documents would ideally help tip the scale in one direction or another. Some had to fight the temptation to make a simple judgment call on a gut level, either in favor of the underdog or against greedy lawyers trying to exploit an unfair opening against a wealthy, well-respected company.

During these two days, Jane's condition clearly took a severe turn for the worse. Phil made the call and activated the home hospice care. A nurse and a nurse's assistant were present on twenty-four-hour watch. She hadn't eaten for four days, and her vital signs were plummeting. The color of her skin, the lack of urination, and the sudden evacuation of her bowels were all indicators that her organs were in the throes of shutting down. For those forty-eight hours, she had only fleeting moments of wakefulness, giving a nod or a squeeze of a hand to her husband and children. The morphine she was given gave her the semblance of peacefulness and absence of any signs of pain but was also assisting her end. Her breathing was strained and measured with an audible gasp at each exhale, her mouth gaping open with a fearsome grimace, struggling for every available molecule of oxygen.

Recovering from the exhaustion of his trip west, Neal quickly submerged himself back into the routine of his life. Truth be told, he didn't give much conscious thought to Jane and her case. After their brief meeting on the sidewalk, it was as if it had been completely purged from his mind. To him, it was just an unpleasant task in his job, like there was in almost any job. "You got to take the good with the bad," he always rationalized to himself.

Just as Phil had thought about euthanizing the family pet when contemplating calling the hospice, Neal regarded his situation in a similar way. He thought about his beloved dog's veterinarian, who worked with all the cute puppies and kittens and received so much gratitude from loving owners like him. The vets, too, had the horrible task of putting those same animals to sleep when it was their time. Confronting the heartbroken, grieving families, the vet had to buck up and be professional and not get too emotionally involved. It was about doing the right thing to end needless, hopeless pain and suffering. Neal felt justified that he, too, was performing a heroic deed in killing off a threat to the health and well-being of his company.

On the third morning after two final hours of deliberations, the jury rang the buzzer to signal to the bailiff that they had reached a verdict. That same morning, Neal sent in his letter notifying his company that he had decided to retire. And later that afternoon, Jane took her shallow last breath.

AFTERWORD

In a case like Jane's, more often than not, the jury would come back with a decision for the plaintiff and the awarding of substantial compensation, usually in the millions of dollars.

In our story, the jury was finally convinced that the cosmetic talcum powder manufacturers had hidden the most important facts regarding the potential to cause these deadly diseases. Their focus was on making money, the bottom line, and they cared little for their customers. When confronted with the evidence of the product causing disease, they denied their product had asbestos and continued to state that the talcum powder was 100 percent safe.

Decisions such as the one we describe here through Jane's story have forced some of the companies to settle many of the cases and/or make changes to their products. The concept of settling these cases also makes it possible not to admit that there was any wrongdoing. Even today, at least one company is still making claims that their product is 100 percent safe despite agreeing to remove it from the shelves of stores when their supply is depleted.

For well over one hundred years, talc has been mined and used in many products. It was, however, known medically from the 1940s that talc was a cause of granulomatous type fibrosis of the lung. If breathed in large quantities, much like coal miners' lung, people will get this granulomatous disease. It had been called a pneumoconiosis and generally grouped with other types of breathed particles and substances that caused fibrotic lung diseases.

As stated in the beginning of the book, cosmetic talcum powder has been used since ancient times. It has also been known that the talc mines contained veins of asbestos. There was little to no control or even caring on the part of the owners and workers in these mines to test for the presence of the asbestos, primarily because it had not been attributed to the causation of lung fibrosis, tumor development, or mesotheliomas.

That changed in the late 1950s and 60s when Dr. Irving Selikoff, a physician at the Mount Sinai Hospital in New York, conducted a study for the insulators' union. He determined that the asbestos insulation was causing lung fibrosis, lung tumors, and tumors of the pleura called mesotheliomas in the men who were working with this material.

By the end of the '60s, Dr. Selikoff had convinced the government agencies that the use of asbestos in all the products must be stopped because it was basically a poison that was killing the people working with it. Federal, state, and local governments enacted protections for these workers starting around 1974 and banned its use. This was the beginning of significant research looking into whether it was in fact asbestos that caused the diseases and the mechanisms of how it caused the diseases. This research is still ongoing because as we learn more about how tissues and cells work, it leads to more precise knowledge about how the fibrosis or a tumor develops in response to asbestos.

It wasn't until the early1970s that Drs. Arthur Rohl and Arthur Langer started looking at commercially available talcum powders and found by both light microscopic techniques and electron microscopic techniques that the talc was contaminated with asbestos. They published their results, but to a large degree, their findings were totally ignored by the companies that produced the cosmetic talc, as well as the many other products that had talc as an added ingredient (examples include sheetrock, joint compound, and hobby ceramics clay, just to name a few).

In the early 2000s, there was a noticeable increase in the development of mesotheliomas in women. It was still less than what was seen in men who worked with asbestos. Regardless, there was no direct evidence of asbestos exposure except in those women who cleaned the clothes of household members who worked with asbestos-containing products or via secondary exposures. Up to 70 percent of all mesothelioma cases were therefore termed idiopathic (no identifiable cause).

That all began to change around 2005, when it became evident to lawyers who were investigating causes of mesotheliomas that the great majority of these women had exposure only to cosmetic talcum powders. It was then that laboratories began looking at the containers of cosmetic talcum powders to determine if there was asbestos contaminating the talcum powder. Concurrently, many scientists and environmental labs were in fact finding asbestos in the talcum powders and began publishing their findings, supporting the findings of Drs. Rohl and Langer from the early to mid '70s. This even included positive tests by the FDA. These findings explained the high percentage of women developing mesotheliomas with no evidence of having direct or secondary exposures to commercial asbestos. It was also determined that the exposures were generally shown to be primarily contaminating amphibole type asbestos and not the typical amosite and crocidolite used commercially.

The companies that produced the cosmetic talc products fought tooth and nail, saying that they there was no asbestos in their products, denying the findings of environmental labs. Their claim was that the mining companies tested and did not find any, and they tested their products as well with the same results.

In the 1990s, researchers began looking at the use of cosmetic talcum powder and the correlation with ovarian cancer. Numerous studies have shown that the talc and its contaminating asbestos can reach the ovaries of humans when applied to the inguinal regions. Many have correlated the use of talcum powder with the development of ovarian tumors. Although there is somewhat less evidence than mesotheliomas for attribution to ovarian cancer, the data is still extremely convincing. As a result, there have been many lawsuits initiated for cosmetic talcum powder as a cause of ovarian cancer as well.

The companies' arguments were weakened when confronted in court with a paper trail of internal documents confirming that they in fact knew there was asbestos in their products. One specific company was revealed in the early to mid '70s to have modified the manner in which they processed the talc to decrease the amount of asbestos in their product. In court under oath, they also admitted that they only used light microscopic methods to identify if there was asbestos present, knowing full well that it could not be detected by those methods based on amount present and the size of the asbestos fibers. They deliberately hid behind the cosmetic industries' criteria for testing, which was not adequate.

The lawsuits started slowly beginning in the early 2000s with very good results for the plaintiffs who were sick; they were given very high rewards by juries. It was a rare occasion that the defendant companies won a case. It was also true that in almost every case that the defense lost, they would appeal their cases, still claiming that there was no asbestos in their products.

More recently, the companies began to try to settle the cases for significantly less money than the juries were awarding. One of the companies that had been sued early in the process got out of the business of selling its popular talc product and removed it long ago from the shelves. However, another major company finally agreed to take their talcum powder off the market in the US and Canada when the supplies are gone. However, they still put ads in every newspaper in the country and on TV saying that their talcum powder was and is 100 percent safe. To make matters worse, they continue to sell asbestos-tainted talc products overseas in countries that have far lesser regulatory oversight.

The most important message as a takeaway from this book is that all those men and women who have used cosmetic talcum powder and makeup should consider consulting their physician and be monitored for ovary cancer, abdominal and pleural mesotheliomas, and lung tumors.

The fight goes on!

REFERENCES

1976. "Asbestos Fibers Found in Baby Powder." *Washington Post*. March 8.

1976. "Asbestos Found in Ten Powders." *New York Times*. March 10.

Block, L., et al. 2014. "Modernization of Asbestos Testing in USP Talc, U.S. Pharmacopeial Convention, Stimuli to the Revision Process." http://www.usppf.com/pf/pub/data/v404/GEN_STIMULI_404_s201184.html.

Blount, A.M. 1991. "Amphibole Content of Cosmetic and Pharmaceutical Talcs." *Environmental Health Perspectives* 94: 225–230.

"Cancer Facts & Figures 2018—Special Section: Ovarian Cancer." Cancer.org. https://www.cancer.org/content/dam/cancer-org/research/cancer-facts-and-statistics/annual-cancer-facts-and-figures/2018/cancer-facts-and-figures-special-section-ovarian-cancer-2018.pdf.

Cralley, J. 1968. "Fibrous and Mineral Content of Cosmetic Talcum Products," *Amer. Ind. Hyg. Assoc.* July-August 350–354.

Cramer DW, Welch WR, et al. 1982. "Ovarian Cancer and Talc," Cancer 50: 372–376.

Crane D.T. 2019. "Report of Evaluation of Cosmetics and Cosmetic Talc for FDA, U.S. Dept. Labor," Occupational Safety and Health, Salt Lake Technical Center.

Dodson, Ronald F., et al. 2001. "Asbestos content of omentum and mesentery in nonoccupationally exposed individuals," Toxicology and Industrial Health 17:138–143.

Dressen W, Dalla Valle J.M. 1935. "The Effects of Exposure to Dust in Two Georgia Talc Mills and Mines," Public Health Reports 50.

Egilman D, Steffen J, Tran T, Clancy K, Rigler M, Longo. 2019. "Health Effects of Censored Elongated Mineral Particles: A Critical Review." ASTM International.

Emory T.S., Maddox J.C., Kradin R.L. 2020. "Malignant mesothelioma following repeated exposures to cosmetic talc: A case series of 75 patients." American Journal of Industrial Medicine.

EPA: Health Assessment for Talc (March 1992)

Finkelstein, M. 2012. "Malignant Mesothelioma Incidence Among Talc Miners and Millers in New York State," Am J Indust Med 55: 863–868.

Ghio, A, Roggli, V, 2001. "Talc Should Not Be Used for Pleurodesis in Patients with Nonmalignant Pleural Effusions," Am J Respir Crit Care Med 164: 1741.

Gordon, R.E. et al. 2014. "Asbestos in commercial cosmetic talcum powder as a cause of mesothelioma in women," International Journal of Occupational and Environmental Health 4:318–332.

Graham J, Graham R. 1967. "Ovarian cancer and asbestos," Environ Research 1:115–8.

Heller DS, et al. 1996. "Asbestos exposure and ovarian fiber burden," Am J Ind Med 29:435–9.

Henderson W.J., Joslin C.A., Turnbull A.C., Griffiths K. 1971. "Talc and carcinoma of the ovary and cervix," J Obstet Gynaecol Br Commonwealth 78:299–72.

Hillerdal G. 1999. "Mesothelioma: cases associated with non-occupational and low dose exposures," Occup Environ Med 56:505–513.

Hull, M., el at. 2002. "Mesothelioma Among Workers in Asbestiform Fiber-bearing Talc Mines in New York State," Ann. Occup. Hyg., 46, Supplement 1, 132–135.

Interagency Working Group on Asbestos in Consumer Products (IWGACP) publishes "Executive Summary, Preliminary Recommendations on Testing Methods for Asbestos in Talc and Consumer Products Containing Talc," January 6, 2020.

International Conference on Monitoring and Surveillance of Asbestos-Related Diseases. The Helsinki Declaration on Management and Elimination of Asbestos-Related Diseases. Espoo, Finland: Finnish institute of Occupational Health; 2014.

Kadry Taher M, Farhat N, Karyakina N.A. 2019, "Critical review of the association between perineal use of talc powder and risk of ovarian cancer," Reprod Toxicol. 28;90:88–101.

Kleinfeld, M., et al. 1973. "A Study of Workers Exposed to Asbestiform Minerals in Commercial Talc Manufacture," Environ Research 6, 132–143.

Kleinfeld, M. 1967, "Mortality Among Talc Miners and Millers in New York State," Arch Environ. Health, 14:663–667.

Kleinfeld, M., et al. 1955, "Talc Pneumoconiosis, AMA Archives of Industrial Health," 12:66–72.

Kradin R.L., Eng G, Christiani D.C. 2017, "Diffuse peritoneal mesothelioma: A case series of 62 patients including paraoccupational exposures to chrysotile asbestos," American journal of Industrial Medicine. 60:963–7.

Lacourt A, Gramond C, Rolland P, et al. 2014, "Occupational and non-occupational attributable risk of asbestos exposure for malignant pleural meosthelioma," Thorax 69:532–9.

Lamm, S.H., et al. 1988, "Similarities in Lung Cancer and Respiratory Disease Mortality of Vermont and New York State Talc Workers," Epidemiology-Fibers, 1576–1581.

Langseth H & Kjaerheim K. 2004, "Ovarian cancer and occupational exposure among pulp and paper employees in Norway," Scand J Work Environ Health. 30: 356–361.

Langseth H, Hankinson SE, Siemiatycki J, et al. 2008, "Use of talc and risk of ovarian cancer," J Epidemiol Community Health, 62:358-60.

Longo D.K., Young R.S. 1979, "Cosmetic Talc and Ovarian Cancer," The Lancet, 349–351.

Madigan, D., Egilman, D., Finkelstein, M., et al. (2019), "Response to Marsh, G. M., Ierardi, A. M., Benson, S. M., & Finley, B. L. (2019)," "Occupational exposures to cosmetic talc and risk of mesothelioma: an updated pooled cohort and statistical power analysis with consideration of latency period," Inhalation Toxicology, 31:213–223.

Markowitz S. 2015, "Asbestos-Related Lung Cancer and Malignant Mesothelioma of the Pleura: Selected Current Issues," Semin Respir Crit Care Med, 36:334–346.

Millman N. 1947, "Pneumonoconiosis Due To Talc In The Cosmetic Industry," Occup. Med., 4:391.

Moline J, Bevilacqua K, Alexandri M, Gordon R.E. 2020, "Mesothelioma Associated with the Use of Cosmetic Talc," J Occup Environ Med. 62:11-17.

Moskowitz R. 1970, "Talc Pneumoconiosis: A Treated Case, Chest," Vol. 58.

Nam K, Gracey D.R. 1972, "Pulmonary talcosis from cosmetic talcum powder," JAMA. 31;221(5):492–3.

Paoletti, L. 1984, "Evaluation by Electron Microscopy Techniques of Asbestos Contamination in Industrial, Cosmetic and Pharmaceutical Talcs," Regulatory Toxicology and Pharmacology, 4:222–235.

Reid A, Klerk N, Musk A.W. 2011, "Does Exposure to Asbestos Cause Ovarian Cancer? A Systematic Literature Review and Meta-analysis," Cancer Epidemiol Biomarkers Prev. 20: 1287–1295.

Rohl, A.N. 1974, "Asbestos in Talc," Enviro Health Persp, 9:129–132.

Rohl A.N., Langer A, 1974, "Identification and Quantitation of Asbestos in Talc," Enviro Health Persp, 9:95–109.

Rohl, A., Langer, A., et al. 1976, "Consumer Talcums and Powders: Mineral and Chemical Characterization," Journal of Toxicology and Environmental Health, 2:255–284.

Rosner, D., et al. 2019, ""Nondetected": The Politics of Measurement of Asbestos in Talc," 1971–1976, Public Health Then and Now, AJPH, Vol. 109.

Selevan S.G., Dement J.M. 1979, "Mortality Patterns Among Miners and Millers of Non-Asbestiform Talc: Preliminary Report," Journal of Environmental Pathology and Toxicology, Vol. 2.

Snider, D., et al. 1972, "Asbestosform Impurities In Commercial Talcum Powders," The Compass of Sigma Gamma Epsilon, Vol. 49.

Srebo S, Roggli, V, 1994, "Asbestos-Related Disease Associated with Exposure to Asbestiform Tremolite," Am J Int Med 26, 809–819.

Steffen J.E., Tran T, Yimam M, et al. 2019, "Serous Ovarian Cancer Caused by Exposure to Asbestos in Cosmetic Talc Powders – A Case Series," JOEM.

Terry K.L., Karageorgi S, Shvetsov Y.B., et al. 2013, "Genital powder use and risk of ovarian cancer: a pooled analysis of 8525 cases and 9859 controls." Cancer Prev Res 6:811–821.

Van Gosen, Bradley, The Geology of Asbestos in the United States and Its Practical Applications, Environmental & Engineering Geoscience, Vol. XIII, No. 1, February 2007. pp. 55–63.

Van Gosen, Bradley, et al. 2004, "Using the geologic setting of talc deposits as an indicator of amphibole asbestos content," Environmental Geology 920–939.

Venter P.F., Iturralde M. 1979, "Migration of a particulate radioactive tracer from the vagina to the peritoneal cavity and ovaries." S Afr Med J. 2;55:917–9.

Welch, Laura, et al. 2005, "Asbestos and Peritoneal Mesothelioma among College-educated Men," International Journal of Occupational Environmental Health 11: 254–258.

www.ingramcontent.com/pod-product-compliance
Lightning Source LLC
LaVergne TN
LVHW041812060526
838201LV00046B/1230